HOME SWEET HOME

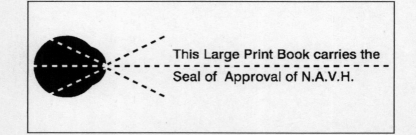

This Large Print Book carries the
Seal of Approval of N.A.V.H.

HOME SWEET HOME

KIM WATTERS

THORNDIKE PRESS
A part of Gale, Cengage Learning

GALE
CENGAGE Learning·

Detroit • New York • San Francisco • New Haven, Conn • Waterville, Maine • London

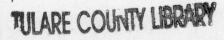

GALE
CENGAGE Learning®

LIBRARY OF CONGRESS CATALOGING-IN-PUBLICATION DATA

Watters, Kim.
    Home sweet home / by Kim Watters. — Large print ed.
      p. cm. — (Thorndike Press large print Christian fiction)
    ISBN-13: 978-1-4104-4374-8(hardcover)
    ISBN-10: 1-4104-4374-4(hardcover)
    1. Bed and breakfast accommodations—Fiction. 2.
Contractors—Fiction. 3. Large type books.
PS3623.A877H68 2011
813'.6—dc23   2011036186

Published in 2012 by arrangement with Harlequin Books S.A.

Printed in Mexico
1 2 3 4 5 6 7 16 15 14 13 12

Do not judge,
and you will not be judged.
Do not condemn,
and you will not be condemned.
Forgive, and you will be forgiven.
— *Luke* 6:38

For Shane and Emily, the loves of my life who don't quite grasp the concept yet that these books don't write themselves, and my sister, Karin Roepel, and my mom, Sharon Galitz, who made sure it all made sense.

CHAPTER ONE

"Do not judge, and you will not be judged. Do not condemn, and you will not be condemned. Forgive, and you will be forgiven."

— Luke 6:37

"This is it?" Wide-eyed and a little confused, Abby Bancroft stared out the passenger side window of the Ford Escort parked in front of the large Victorian house. Her stomach churned as her gaze flipped between the obviously outdated brochure in her cold hand and the three-story wooden structure to her right in need of a new paint job and some other cosmetic work. If the outside reflected the inside, her vision of reopening the Bancroft Bed-and-Breakfast by the Founder's Day Festival the first weekend in May died a quick and painful death.

Disappointment pooled around her shoulders and matched the dismal early March

9

skies. Puffy gray clouds threatened more snow in the sleepy town of Dynamite Creek in northern Arizona. The bare limbs of the tree standing guard by the long porch running along the front of the house looked more inviting than the empty windows that stared back at her. She should have guessed the house would be as welcoming as the people who once lived inside.

"Yep. This is it. We're here." Delia Wentworth, the receptionist from her late grandmother's attorney's office unbuckled her seat belt and opened the driver's side door. Frigid air blew through the interior, making Abby shiver inside her inadequate jacket and miss the warm Southern California weather. *Here* wasn't exactly the picture perfect place she'd expected to find as she sat frozen inside the car.

"It's really a great house. It just needs a little TLC," Delia responded enthusiastically before leaving the car.

"A little?" Abby's skepticism showed in her voice. She knew nothing about general construction, but she had eyes, unless something in her brain had gone haywire in the long drive between Los Angeles and Dynamite Creek. Maybe she needed a pair of rose-colored glasses like Delia wore because Abby didn't quite see the old

Victorian in the same way.

Pulling her collar around her neck, Abby grabbed her purse, exited the car and walked to where the young woman stood. Abby held up the brochure and compared it with the house. Then she flipped the piece of paper over. The photo credit was from 1987. Figures. Over the years, beautiful and welcoming had morphed into dismal and uninviting. The yellow paint had faded over time and had begun to peel in several places and some of the porch railing sagged. And that was just what she could see.

A gust of wind frosted her legs and whipped a loose strand of hair into her eyes. Abby should have waited until May to collect her inheritance, but the letter from the attorney's office hadn't really given her much choice and she wasn't fool enough to walk away from a place she could finally call home. If she found a way to fit into Dynamite Creek.

The cold, hard reality in front of her caused doubt to creep in. She didn't have a lot of money or time for a place that wasn't turnkey, but she'd never be able to reopen the B and B until it resembled the picture in her hand. Her gaze skimmed the dull, faded exterior again. No one in his or her right mind would even consider staying in

11

the house in its present condition. How the Bancrofts managed to attract customers the past few years amazed her. Even though the home had only been shut down six months ago with their deaths, neglect clung to every nook and cranny.

"Okay, the place needs more than just a little bit of care. Your grandparents —"

"Charles and Sally Bancroft?" Bitterness and disappointment pulsed in her heart. "Hardly. Grandparents only by name." Crossing her arms in front of her, she stared at the numbers screwed to the fence post also in need of a fresh coat of paint.

The Bancrofts hadn't cared that her mother, Sharon, had spent years working two jobs and struggling to make ends meet while raising their granddaughter. Nor had they bothered to visit while her mother was ill. They hadn't even gone to her funeral when her mother finally succumbed to cancer ten years earlier. How apropos they'd saddle Abby with a falling down pile of wood that was probably as cold on the inside as it looked on the outside.

"Well, the Bancrofts had hired a contracting firm out of Phoenix with roots from Dynamite Creek to remodel the place about a year ago, but one of the partners took off with the hefty deposit money and never started the job." Delia opened the gate and ushered Abby through. "That pretty much destroyed them physically and emotionally. Your grandfather died shortly afterward from a heart attack. Your grandmother didn't last too much longer. Such a shame. Anyway, as my boss told you, aside from the house, there wasn't much left once their medical bills were satisfied. Come on, let me show you the interior."

Not much left was right. Abby guessed she had two months of inheritance money to survive plus what she'd stocked away in savings and her retirement fund. She had to open the B and B or be forced to accept another failure. Maybe she should sell the property? But who would buy the run-down place in this economy? And did she really want to walk away from where her mother grew up? Houses like this didn't fall from the sky every day. Not for her anyway.

Following the younger blonde up the walkway, Abby's gaze skimmed the brown patches of grass peeking through the thin layer of old snow. Dead garden beds lined the sidewalk and the base of the house. Only the partially visible green shrubbery showed any signs of life.

"You were their legal firm, why didn't you sue?" The wooden steps creaked under her weight and the metal handrail only numbed her hand further. Bare branches rustled in the wind and dead leaves sounded nothing like the waves pounding against the shore of her favorite place in L.A. Dirt and debris piled on the porch looked nothing like the soft, grainy sand on the beach where she used to work as a teenager.

"Mrs. Bancroft didn't want to. I think she had a soft spot for the partner left holding the proverbial bag, but it wouldn't have mattered anyway. The company filed bankruptcy." Unlocking the front door, Delia stepped through and flipped the light switch. "I'll bring over the contract and bankruptcy paperwork later if you'd like."

"That's not necessary. I doubt I'll ever run into any of them, so I won't be able to give them a piece of my mind," Abby replied as she stepped inside. The warm interior surprised her, as did the lighting from the old-fashioned stained-glass light suspended from the foyer ceiling. "Heat? Electricity?"

"I'll bring it by anyway. My boss turned on the utilities yesterday for your arrival. In anticipation of your continuing the business, he even managed to get the phone service activated as of this morning under the Bancroft Bed-and-Breakfast name. Don't be surprised if you start getting calls for reservations. Despite how it looks, the Bancrofts had standing reservations every year for the Founder's Day Festival. Aside from this one, there's only two other B and B's in town, and they're probably already full. There's a file folder on the kitchen table with all the contact numbers so you can switch everything into your name. It's right this way."

Abby trailed after Delia, feeling as if she'd stepped back in time. A crystal chandelier hung from the center of the long hall, the light merrily reflecting off the glass. A tall wooden chair with a beveled mirror that also doubled as a coat rack graced the faded wall by the fireplace. High doorways on either side of the foyer led to more rooms. Beneath her feet, small, multicolored tile peeked out from underneath the worn rug. Despite the scent of neglect, the house had a charm she could almost grow accustomed to. She spun around, trying to take it all in before she hustled after the other woman. At a first glance, the interior needed as much work as the exterior, especially the kitchen. It was way too small.

Her heart plummeted again as enormous dollar signs flashed in her brain. She'd have to take out a loan. The appliances looked like they hadn't been updated since the late sixties. The lime green, orange and gold linoleum flooring had to go, but the Formica dinette table showed promise. It reminded her of Mrs. White's, the elderly woman who lived in the apartment next door to Abby's last place of residence.

"Here's the information on the utilities." Delia handed her the folder from the table. "And I thought you might appreciate this." The assistant handed her another folder — a thicker one with several pamphlets inside. "It's kind of like a welcome packet. I know what it's like being new to town having moved here a few years ago with my husband, so I stopped by the Chamber of Commerce and got you this stuff. There's also some information about the church we belong to in case you're looking."

Church. Another concept as foreign as the small town of Dynamite Creek. The only time she'd ever stepped foot in one was for her mother's funeral. Not wanting to hurt Delia's feelings, Abby took the folder. Aside from the church, the rest of the information inside could prove useful. "Thanks. I'll be sure to look everything over when I get the chance."

Frigid air swirled around them as they walked back to Delia's car, the piercing wind sneaking inside Abby's collar. She

16

shivered and got inside to go back to the attorney's office. Determination filled her when she glanced at the house again. Her mother had once told Abby that hard physical work brought rewards beyond compare. It looked like Abby was finally getting her chance to see if her mother's wisdom rang true. And maybe she'd finally found the home she'd always been searching for.

The sound of the phone woke Abby from a deep sleep. Stretching in the dim dawn light, she unwound her stiff body from the sofa where she'd sat down to rest just after midnight. Her brain still full of cobwebs, she stumbled to the back room she'd discovered yesterday while exploring the place. She grabbed the phone on the antique desk before she turned on the stained-glass lamp. A kaleidoscope of color danced across her vision as light spilled over the dark patch of stain on the desk that hadn't been worn thin like the rest of the surface. "Hello?"

"Hello?" A woman's voice floated over the line. "Is this the Bancroft Bed-and-Breakfast?"

Dread and a tinge of anticipation chased away her exhaustion. Abby found a stray curl and wound it around her pointer finger. Breathing deeply, she stilled the butterflies

17

whirling in her stomach. "Yes. Sorry. This is the Bancroft Bed-and-Breakfast, how may I help you?"

"Yes. We'd like to make a reservation."

Abby's eyes widened at the sight of the old-fashioned black rotary phone. She didn't even know these things existed anymore outside of the movies. The numbering in the circles even looked foreign to her like most of the antiques inside the house.

"Um. Sure." With her computer still in a box on the floor next to the desk, Abby searched frantically for a piece of paper to write her first customer's information on. Her hand stilled on what looked like an old ledger stuffed inside the top drawer. Blowing lightly to clear the dust, she placed it on the worn surface and yanked a pen from the holder next to the lamp, her hands damp with a bit of nervous moisture. A lump formed in her throat but she managed to find her voice. "Our reopening will be May 5. Or would you be looking for a date later in the summer?"

"Hang on a moment. Harry, I've managed to get a hold of someone. It looks like we can get our Founder's Day Weekend after all." Abby held the phone away from her ear as the woman conversed with her husband.

Her gaze froze on the peeling corner of dark orange wallpaper with silver and gold thread running through it. She closed her eyes and dropped her forehead to rest on the palm of her left hand. What was she doing? There was no way she was going to get this house in order to receive guests in two months' time. Not without help and considering she knew no one in town except Delia and her boss, no one would be coming to her aid any time soon. Her breath rushed out in one big whoosh, sending a dust bunny fluttering to the floor along with her confidence.

"Fine. We'll take that weekend. We always love coming to The Founder's Day Festival. This is Harry and Edith Gordon. And we always stay in the blue room. This is Sally, right?"

Abby paused a moment and furrowed her brow. Making sure she said the right thing was as important as making sure she correctly wrote the information down in the faded yellow ledger. "No, this is her granddaughter, Abby. I'm sorry to say that both Charles and Sally passed away last year."

"Oh, how sad. I'm so sorry, dear. Funny, they never mentioned you, though."

She almost snapped the pen in two as she wrote in the date on the first available space she could find. "You'll still be coming, won't you?"

"As long as you don't give us some ridiculous rate or change things too much. We're creatures of habit, you know. And we hope you know how to make those blueberry scones your grandmother was famous for."

Biting her lip, Abby nodded until she realized the woman couldn't see her reaction. "Of course, Mrs. Gordon. Your rate will be the same as last year since you're a repeat customer. I'll be taking care of a few repairs and painting and such, but everything else should be pretty much as you remember it. Thank you for staying with us again. Have a nice day."

After hanging up the phone, more butterflies gathered in her stomach. What kind of businesswoman was she? Not a very good one. She'd been a lifeguard, a waitress, a store clerk, a pizza delivery girl and had worked in an insurance office. The few business classes she'd taken in junior college hadn't prepared her for the real world. Figuring out how to make blueberry scones was the least of her problems. She hadn't secured the room with a credit card or gotten any of the Gordons' contact information. Hopefully her grandparents had been good bookkeepers.

Soft sunlight filtered in through the slats of the old wooden blinds as she sat at the desk. The chair squeaked in disapproval as she leaned back. Bookshelves and file cabinets filled the entire side wall. It would probably take until May to figure out what rate the Gordons' had paid last year, especially since the only technology in the room seemed to be the calculator by the memo pad.

On a whim, she paged through the ledger and breathed in a hint of lilacs. Her fingers traced her grandmother's writing. The flowery loops and swirls made her wonder what type of woman wore that scent or wrote with such flourish. Nothing indicated the image of the hardened bitter woman that Abby associated with the name Sally Bancroft.

Closing the book, Abby pushed back the chair and stood. No time to waste another minute. After she drank some coffee and went for her morning run, she had a computer to set up, a house to get in order, and more customers to find to fill the rooms. With the Gordon reservation, there was no turning back now.

Cole Preston stepped out of his battered white pickup truck and almost slipped on the patch of ice. Pain shot up his arm when the side of his palm connected with the cold metal of his driver's side door. Not exactly a good way to start his final obligation but he wouldn't turn back now like he had the first time when he'd discovered the elderly Bancrofts had died.

No, his twin sister, Christine, who still lived here, had told him yesterday a granddaughter had taken up residence, and he'd returned immediately. Once he finished with the restorations of the Bancroft place, the town might not see him as a crook and his dignity would be restored. Hopefully.

He winced. Guilty by association. Cole had known about Robert's gambling problem, and tried to quietly intervene, but without success. He would have never believed his partner of ten years would run off with the company money and assets and leave such a mess in his wake.

But he wasn't one to judge. Only God could do that.

Straightening his back, he slammed the door, and then turned and leaned against it, careful to make sure his feet stayed clear of the ice. The air squeezed from his lungs. He remembered this house and the people who'd lived inside. While Mr. Bancroft had been sour and gruff, his wife was one of the few people who'd treated him with decency when he'd worked for them in his youth. He wondered what the granddaughter would be like.

The monstrosity across the street gaped at him with its blank windows and peeling paint. His ex-partner had been crazy to take on a project this size without consulting him, but then again, Robert had never had any intention of actually doing the job in the first place. He just wanted the money that came with it. The Bancrofts had come to their company because Cole had been a local. Bile found a spot at the back of his throat. His partner's actions had erased his good name from the all the directories in Dynamite Creek.

He rubbed his eyes. Leaving Phoenix before dawn to make the two-hour drive north to the mountains had caught up with him. Not that he slept much anyway these days. That would change when he finished the Bancroft place. He would be able to hold his head high again. His gaze scraped the exterior a second time. Or maybe he'd have to slink away with his tail between his legs because he didn't trust his own judgment anymore.

Gingerly making his way across the empty street, he paused in front of the white picket fence in need of paint and took in the glow of the sun rising behind the house. A clear, bright sky that promised another glorious day had begun.

A light turned on in the front part of the house, accentuating the stained-glass squares at the top of the large bay window, but he couldn't see the person who flipped the switch. His watch said eight in the morning. At least the new owner wasn't a night owl that slept half the day away, which would make part of his job easier if he could start at a decent hour. The part of his brain that could still think told him to go back into town and grab another cup of coffee from Sunrise Diner and catch up on the local gossip. The other part made his hand move to open the gate, and his feet to march down the cracked sidewalk, up the creaky stairs and across the recently swept porch.

He was here. The sooner he started, the sooner he'd finish. His lips pursed. As long as the interior was in better shape than the exterior he might be done by the end of summer.

"Okay, Lord, I need You to have my back here." His words hung in the clear, fresh air. A few years into his new faith, Cole still found it hard to ask for help when he needed it but God's love had helped him through the darkest times with his partner's betrayal and would continue to do so.

Cole pushed his finger on the doorbell, not surprised he couldn't hear the chime inside the house. He shifted his weight. At least that would be an easy fix. After rapping his bare knuckles on the wood section beneath the inlaid glass in the door, he shoved his bruised hand inside his jacket pocket and waited.

After a few moments of struggling with the lock, the person on the other side finally opened the front door a crack and half a face stared back at him. Wisps of curly, blond hair escaped from the red bandanna tied around her head, but the deep green eyes held him spellbound and unsure of his next action. "Ms. Bancroft?"

Hesitation fell over the woman's fatigued expression. "Yes."

"Good morning." That cup of coffee sounded better and better, especially when he smelled the telltale aroma of the brewing liquid coming from somewhere behind the woman. He should have gone to the diner

25

and asked some questions. Except he knew the moment he stepped inside, he would be the topic of everyone's conversation.

"Good morning. May I help you?"

Cold seeped through the open neck of Cole's jacket. What he wouldn't give to get out of the bitter snowy mountains and retreat *down the hill* back to Phoenix. Too many years he'd spent the winters shoveling people's driveways, the frigid temperatures chapping his hands and cheeks because all his money went to help his mother so he hadn't been able to afford gloves or a scarf. Snow was only good for sledding and even then, he left it behind him after he finished with the hills. Until he fixed the wrong his ex-partner had done though, he was stuck in Dynamite Creek.

His sister would be happy. His mother wouldn't even care.

"I'm Cole Preston. I . . ." His tongue refused to work as he stared at her. The young woman — only a few years younger than him — didn't resemble either of the elderly Bancrofts he'd remembered from his youth, and he had no idea what their daughter had looked like because she'd run away when only eighteen years old which was before Cole was born.

Silence expanded between them. Cole

took a step back. His fists clenched inside the pockets of his jacket. He turned at the sound behind him. A lone jogger ran by on the sidewalk, his warm breath fanning in the still morning air. The man's attention stayed on Cole until they made eye contact and Cole recognized him. Mr. Turner turned away without acknowledging him. Small town living hadn't changed. He couldn't wait to escape again.

Coming back had been another error in his judgment and the weight of the couple's death surrounded him in a pile of guilt. Determination pushed away his sudden insecurities. He had a job to do albeit several months past the deadline.

"Mr. Preston, what did you need? I've got a lot to do today." The woman blinked.

Cole's heart sunk along with the promise of the new day. He heard a car slow down as it passed by and his ears burned. In the distance, a dog howled, as if mocking his attempt to move on with his life. "I'm here to fulfill the contract your grandparents signed with Preston Restorations to remodel the house. May I come in?"

The inviting scent of coffee still drifted past his nostrils. Too bad the woman didn't complement the aroma inside the house. "So you're the contractor that bailed out on my grandparents. You're finally here to fix the house? A little late, aren't you? You really have a lot of nerve coming back here after everything that's happened. Why, I ought to —"

Cole bent his head in frustration and clenched his fingers. Instead of finishing this project first, he'd saved it for last, choosing to do the other contracts in order of signing date. He'd hoped to retreat back to Dynamite Creek and rebuild. Instead he faced even more animosity than before he'd left. "I know and I'm sorry. I had my reasons, but I'm here now."

Disappointment pummeled his heart. Coming home had been a mistake.

The woman sighed, deflated as she shook her head. "Look. I'm sorry, too. I had no reason to go off on you like that. I'm tired and a bit overwhelmed right now. Please just take your reasons and go away. I don't need you."

She did need him but she didn't trust him. No surprise there. He didn't trust himself these days but if he wanted to move on, he had to complete this one last job.

Okay, Lord, I really need Your help on this one. "I deserved that and more."

The woman's green eyes intrigued him to the point of distraction. Maybe he should

28

forget about the contract. He didn't owe it to the new owner since he'd closed shop and filed bankruptcy, but he couldn't walk away. He was determined to finish this project so he could move on.

"Yoo-hoo, dearie. Good morning." A voice from the yard cut the stillness.

At the familiarity of that tone, Cole's back stiffened. He knew the owner of those words. He'd shoveled her walk and raked her leaves, too.

A smile spread across the young woman's face, changing her whole demeanor. Cole wondered if he'd ever be on the receiving end of such promise of sunshine on a cloudy day. "Good morning, Mrs. Wendt. Your tuna casserole was delicious. Thanks. We can chat later, okay?"

"You're more than welcome." The voice grew closer. "Oh my goodness. Cole? Cole Preston, is that you?"

Tension pulled his shoulders back. Somehow it didn't surprise him that Mrs. Wendt recognized him after all these years. He turned, pulled up the corners of his lips and waved, willing the elderly woman, the town gossip if his memory didn't fail him, to go back into her house. Cole didn't need an audience to his humiliation. He shifted his weight. His presence was sure to start her lips flapping again. "Good morning, Mrs. Wendt. Nice to see you again."

"You, too, Cole. Welcome home." It figured the one person to welcome him was probably the last person he wanted to see right now. To Cole's relief, the elderly neighbor started down her driveway to retrieve the morning paper, but he also noticed she lingered staring up at them as she tapped the roll against her palm.

Welcome home. What an oxymoron.

Another millisecond passed as he heard the door hinges squeak behind him. Cole swiveled back around in time to see the door open wider. "Fine. Come in then."

"My condolences again on your grandparents." Cole stepped inside.

"Not that it means anything, but thanks."

He shrugged off her nonchalant comment and rubbed the back of his neck with stiff fingers. The heat inside warmed him as his gaze took in the interior. Despite the dingy light and dark green paint and ugly wallpaper, he fell in love with the heavy oak chair rail and the recessed paneling that skirted the room. Some of his apprehension disappeared when he noticed that most of the original corbels and molding remained, as did the double doorways to each of the rooms that fed from the reception area. Too

30

bad everything was covered with layers of paint. The marble fireplace and the partially scraped oak floors looked good compared to replacing the entire porch and stairs outside. Still, the inside needed more cosmetic work than the exterior. He gritted his teeth. He might be done before next Christmas if he hired some outside help. If anyone in town would work for him.

Building a reputation took years, tarnishing it only took days.

"I see Mrs. Wendt still lives here." Winter seeped in through the space under the door.

"Yes." The woman folded her arms under her chest and stared at him, a million questions etched in her very being. Now that he had a full view of her, her honey blond hair peeking out from beneath her scarf was touched with a hint of curl, and made him want to reach out and feel its softness. Incredibly long lashes rimmed her almond shaped eyes and a slight pink tint colored her cheeks. His heartbeat quickened at the sight of the haunted shadows bruising the delicate skin underneath her eyes. "She's one of the many who've welcomed me to town."

"Dynamite Creek's like that." For some. Not for him. Unless he counted Mrs. Wendt.

"So you're from around here then." Fa-

31

tigue laced her voice as she stared up at him. "That's right. Delia mentioned one of the contractors was a local."

Cole fought the impulse to comfort the woman and fix whatever problems troubled her. He was only responsible for the house, not the new owner, and he meant to keep it that way because he had no intention of staying here any longer than necessary. "I grew up a few blocks from here."

The coffeemaker chimed from the kitchen in the back of the house. The woman turned toward the sound, giving Cole a quick view of her long, elegant neck. When she flipped her head back, her long hair bounced from underneath her scarf and settled around her thin shoulders. The freshly shampooed scent joined the aroma of the coffee. Uncertainty furrowed the area between her eyes and the urge to wrap his arms around her confused him. He fixed houses, not people.

"Would you like some coffee?"

Her words lifted his spirits. Maybe today wouldn't be the complete and utter failure it started out to be the moment he set eyes on the house. "That would be great. Thanks."

"Right this way then."

Cole followed her, taking note of the ugly wallpaper and scratched oak floor. Between the two things taking up his vision, Cole's heart couldn't decide whether to beat with anticipation or dread.

"I have to warn you, I don't have any milk or cream because I take mine black." The woman's words grounded him back to the here and now.

"So do I. Why ruin a good cup of java?"

"My sentiments exactly." As she ushered him to the round Formica table in the corner of the kitchen by the bay window, a tiny smile flashed across her full lips.

A few moments later, their fingers touched when she handed him his coffee and a spark crackled between them. They both frowned in unison and stared guardedly at each other. Cole put it down to static electricity, nothing more. He was simply here to fix the house, not to find romance in the town he'd washed his hands of twelve years earlier.

Relationships were for people ready for a permanent commitment and willing to settle down. Something Cole wasn't able to do yet. Unlike his father, Cole wouldn't be trapped into a loveless marriage that ended in divorce, destroying his faith in the institution. Abby took the seat opposite him, placing the table between them. The distance suited him, yet gave him a clear view of her flawless skin, high cheekbones and delicate nose. His heart beat a little faster.

She eyed him above the rim of her cup. "So, Mr. Preston, have you taken a good look around you? Now that you've seen a little bit of what's in store for you, isn't it time to leave?"

Her question troubled him. It was almost as if she expected him to abandon the project. Why? But then again, given the brief history she knew about his defunct company, maybe she knew something he didn't. He'd made some errors in the past, which continued to haunt him.

"The name's Cole. What's your first name?" He sipped the scalding liquid, glad for a way to occupy his hands. Something about the woman intrigued him and despite his reservations about the house, she made him want to linger long after he reached the bottom of his cup.

Hope and another emotion he couldn't identify descended over the woman's features. "You really intend to do the work? Even though the people who signed the contract are dead?"

He set the cup on the table, his grip tightening around the yellow ceramic. He needed to do the remodel so he could start over again somewhere else. "I won't leave until I'm finished."

"But you'll leave. They always do." The plea in her eyes and the softness of her voice chiseled away another piece of the wall surrounding his heart. Even though they just met, he realized that, for the time being, they needed each other.

CHAPTER TWO

"Yes. Contractors usually do leave when the job is done." Cole reached over and placed a calloused hand over her clenched ones. "If you're looking for something more, I'm not the guy."

Abby stared at the man, who wore his dark short hair styled in a way that suited him. Shallow laugh lines touched the corners of his eyes and mouth, and his skin had been lightly kissed by the sun. His quarter-zip light blue sweater accented his shoulders and muscular arms, but it was his earthy brown eyes that captivated her and made her want to dig in and sow the seeds of something more permanent.

His touch warmed and chilled her at the same time. Confused, she pulled back her hands and forced them onto her lap. Good going, girl. Push him away. Make him run for the hills. Cole Preston is the answer to what some would call prayers, but to her it had been a simple plea to the universe. Not only could he help her get the house done in time, he could help her be accepted into Dynamite Creek. If she turned him away, the people might do the same to her and then she'd never fit in or find a real home.

"Of course not. I never suggested you were, Mr. Preston." Abby pulled out her calm facade, something she'd perfected years ago in each new neighborhood, each new school, each time she was ridiculed because of the cheap, discounted chain store clothes she wore.

"Cole. The name's Cole, Ms. Bancroft. What's yours again?" When he grinned, tiny dimples appeared.

Her breathing quickened. He affected her on a different level and in a way she didn't understand in her limited experience with men. "Abby."

"Abby. That suits you. Short for Abigail?"

"Yes." The way he said her first name reminded her of liquid velvet. Her heart fluttered. Abby retreated to the coffeemaker to refill her cup. Distance. That's what she needed. With the crook of an eyebrow or quirk of his lips, the man had the ability to get under her shell.

Turning away from the worn counter, she leaned against it, the edge cutting into her back. Cole had moved from the table and now stood less than three feet from her. An unexplainable intrinsic energy dragged her toward him so she stepped to the side to put more space between them. His nearness plucked at her sanity, pulling it apart one tiny strand at a time until she felt exposed and vulnerable. "How much is this going to cost me?"

"Your grandparents already paid a hefty deposit. Until that's exhausted, the labor is free."

"The labor, but not the materials." *Ka-ching.* Dollar signs blazed inside her brain. With the entire house needing attention, the paint, the flooring, and whatever else this monstrosity required, the labor would probably be the cheap part.

Abby dragged in a ragged gasp and caught a whiff of Cole's aftershave. Masculine with a dash of adventure mixed in. Her pulse accelerated. But she didn't need adventure; she'd had enough of that growing up. Suddenly she didn't want him in her house or anywhere near her because he was dangerous to her peace of mind. If she wasn't careful, she'd find herself falling for another person who had no intention of sticking around in her life.

Indecision clawed at her, tore at her

insides. She had to make this work. Her fingernails bit into her palms as she glanced around the room. Morning sunlight filtered in through the window above the sink and highlighted every flaw and blemish in the kitchen. The rest of the house wasn't any better, but she couldn't get rid of him. Not now when she had only enough income to survive for two months and guests arriving at the beginning of May that expected a decent place to stay.

"We'll work something out. When do I start?" His crooked smile sent her pulses on another one of those road trips her mother had been so fond of. "You won't regret it."

Abby already did. Suddenly, she wanted off of the emotional roller coaster but it was too late. Despite her earlier resolution, Abby decided she was going to be sorry she let Cole into her house and her life for the next few months.

"May as well start today since you're here." Her sigh filled the small area between them, yet when she glanced up, his mocha-colored eyes invited her to sit back and stay awhile. Something she wasn't about to let happen. Until she could identify this crazy thing swirling around them, the more space she kept between them the better. "Even though you've already seen it, let me refresh your memory. You may change your mind."

Abby pushed herself away from the counter and marched past him, grabbing another lungful of his masculinity. Once he realized the scope of the project, he'd probably disappear again. Disappointment made a home in her heart. Just once she'd like to lead a normal life. Just once she'd like to have someone stick around. But even more important, she wanted to find a permanent place to call home.

She stood in the doorway leading into the small kitchen and waited for Cole to catch up. More tension crystallized into tiny fragments of emotional energy when he moved in behind her.

His guarded whisper scraped her eardrums. "Contrary to what you might believe, I've never been inside here before. My ex-partner came and bid on the project and took the money. Until it's paid back, I won't change my mind. After you."

Abby felt the weight of his gaze all the way down the hall. Something weird and crazy seemed to pass between them every time they came in close proximity. Maybe she should get a job? Surely there had to be someone in town who needed help. She had enough experience doing mundane things, and she could use the extra money. That would keep her away during the day, but if she did that, the restorations would take that much longer without her help.

Besides, who would hire Bancroft's illegitimate granddaughter? Sure the people in town had been more than welcoming to her, but for how long? *Don't go there.* Her teeth buried themselves into her bottom lip as she pivoted by the front door. "As you can see, this is the foyer."

"Actually, it's the reception area. People used to mingle here while waiting for dinner to be served. That's why it's wider than a normal hall. I like it, though the wallpaper and paint have to go." Cole walked over to the wood staircase near the back right and ran his hands across the smooth, paint-coated banister that led to the second floor.

"No kidding." Abby crossed her arms again and leaned against the fireplace, a blast of cold air permeating her thin sweater. She shivered uncontrollably, but more from Cole's longing expression as he stared at the railing than from the temperature. "The rest of the house is just as bad, I'm afraid."

"I figured as much, but it's nothing I can't handle." Cole continued to run his fingers along the painted oak. Something about the new owner brought out his need to fix things. Except he'd learned the hard way, he couldn't fix people. He'd tried and look where it landed him; back in his hometown, his name mud, his dreams shattered.

Cole was better off staying away from people and sticking with houses like this one. He loved the old styles, quirks and all, and renovating them was his specialty. Well, smaller ones, not one of the mansions he'd walked by almost twice a day going to and from school. His vision of owning one though had disappeared along with his scant retirement fund when he started undoing the damage caused by his ex-partner. But that was all in the past.

If God wanted him to have a house like this, He'd provide a way for Cole to achieve it.

He continued to stroke the banister, glad for the diversion from his thoughts. Passion infused his voice. "This house is a gem, Abby. We're lucky so much of it has been kept intact, at least in this space. Let's hope the rest of the rooms are the same. If we don't have to replace any of the crown molding, corbels or ceiling medallions, our timeline will have just decreased. Stripping all the wood will probably take the longest. Did you know that underneath this layer of paint a beautiful piece of oak is just waiting to be exposed?"

"But I don't want to replace things, all I want is for you to paint and wallpaper over everything. That's quicker and easier." She started pacing, determination with a hint of hesitation in each deliberate movement.

She glanced at her watch but Cole deduced she was really running through an imaginary calendar in her head. Frustration nipped at him. He wanted to do the job right and in the process uncover the secrets of the attractive woman at the same time he peeled away the layers of paint and faded wallpaper. He'd certainly be here long enough.

He softened his voice and unwillingly pulled his hand from the banister. "You can't want to continue to cover up the beauty of this place. I believe your grandparents wanted to restore the place back to its original state. And that would involve stripping the paint down to the wood and re-staining it."

"I'm not Charles or Sally." Her gaze swept up the long staircase leading to the second level as if trying to see it through his eyes. "I suppose it would look much better, but I don't have the time."

"Why not? What are you going to do with the place?"

"Reopen the Bancroft Bed-and-

Breakfast."

Cole's fingers curled into fists. Like he'd told Abby, this house was a gem and he could see the possibilities. In fact he could almost hear the clink of silverware and the lull of conversations coming from the dining room to his right, or guests sitting in comfortable lounge chairs in front of a roaring fire in the parlor to his left, or better yet, a posse of children clomping down the steps. These types of houses were meant to be lived in. Cherished. Filled with love and laughter. But after being inside its four walls, the spirit of the house needed mending, as well.

"My first guests arrive the Friday of the Founder's Day Festival," she continued and he heard an edge to her voice and saw her stiffen as if daring him to challenge her.

"That's a little over two months away." Incredulous at the deadline, Cole bit down on his tongue. His stomach churned. He owed Abby in a huge way because she was giving him the chance to clear his name. He'd do everything in his power to make sure the house was done in time even if he had to cut corners in not so obvious places and go without sleep during the entire job. "Fine. I'll have it done by the festival."

Abby faced him. Fear, determination, and

what he sensed as abandonment, all warred for dominance in her expression. A faraway look glazed her eyes, yet her backbone remained fused into a rod. Her lips thinned as she pulled them into a grimace before her determined words spilled out. "This place needs to be ready by the end of April. I'll help, too."

"I'd appreciate that." Plus six more people if anyone besides Abby would work for him.

Cole had an idea there was a lot more going on inside her brain than she divulged, but he let it slide. He had two months to draw her out if he wanted to. Especially if they were going to be working side by side during the remodel. A thought that chased away all the moisture from his mouth. He should get in his truck and hightail it back to Phoenix, but he wouldn't walk away from his final obligation. Or Abby.

"Let's take a look at the rest of the house and see what we've got to do." Cole ushered Abby toward the front and into the parlor to the left, making sure to keep three paces behind her. Not only because he sensed she needed the distance, but because he needed it, as well.

His heart sank once he stepped through the double doors. No crown molding remained and the ceiling medallions had been removed. Plus the servant's entryway and back wall had been covered by floor-to-ceiling wood paneling that had not been painted and darkened the room.

"Not very inviting, is it? Especially the mauve paint, the uneven chair rail and the fake brick finish on the fireplace." Abby's words created an instant headache.

Cole rubbed his eyes in hopes that the room would miraculously change when he reopened them. No such luck. This room would take a lot of time to correct. More days than he'd budgeted for, even with Abby's help. "Not inviting at all. This parlor should be the most formal spot in the house and the most beautiful. This is where the guests would wait for the owners while the servants would bring them food and drink. Nothing remains of the original architecture. Okay then, let's see what else we've got."

His optimism elevated a bit at the sight of the wall-to-wall shag carpeting covering the living room's hardwood floors. At least the hideous rug should have protected the oak underneath. And barring any unseen problems, the walls could be covered by a fresh coat of paint, or covered with wallpaper. He pivoted around. More things that showed promise were the original large ornate mantel and fireplace dominating the interior wall and the stained-glass portion of the windows at the top of the panes buried under several layers of paint. The integrity of this room had survived the multiple attempts of remodeling over the years.

"Pretty ghastly, isn't it?" Abby's shoulders slumped and pretty much matched his current mood.

"Actually, it's better than the parlor, but I'm not crazy that they partitioned off the back for an office even though I suppose it was necessary. They could have done a little better job in keeping with the lines of the house." Maybe he should retreat to the kitchen and grab his coffee cup. But the more awake he became, the worse the house would look. Once he pulled up the carpet though, he hoped the floors underneath wouldn't be that bad.

"I have no idea what your ancestors and grandparents were thinking when they changed the interior so much." Cole scratched the back of his neck as he paced around the mismatched furniture interspersed with the antique pieces. With luck, Abby might be able to find some replicas and recover the antiques if she ventured to Phoenix. Maybe his sister could give Abby some ideas with the interior design if he could pry her away from her shop and daughter for a few days.

"You knew them?"

"Of course. Everyone in town did." His fingers touched the cool surface of the fireplace. Solid. Good. He squatted down and stuck his head partially inside. Hopefully it just needed a good cleaning. He pulled his head out and rose to his feet and turned to face her. "I used to shovel their walk, rake the leaves and mow the lawn when I was a kid. Your grandmother always brought me out a cup of hot chocolate or a glass of fresh-squeezed lemonade. Even though we were never allowed inside, she treated me like I was one of the family."

Cole watched the color disappear from her face as she sank down onto the brown couch. A frown marred her pretty features, yet he couldn't hear the mumbled words that passed through her lips. Resisting the urge to cross the carpet and sit down next to her, he thrust his hands into his jean pockets and rocked back and forth on his heels. His fingers found the change left over from his convenience store sandwich bought last night.

Something wasn't right and he sensed he should tread with caution but somehow the question slipped out. "You never came to visit. Why?"

"I didn't know they existed until I inherited this monstrosity."

The regret and bitterness caught him off guard and her green eyes held his captive. Then it hit him, unsettling his nerves. In his brief survey of the room earlier, he saw no family pictures. No heirlooms. No personal items of people that had spent their lives here. Nothing to indicate that this was a home and not just a building with four walls and a roof.

This time he commanded his legs to move and he planted himself on the cushion next to Abby. He picked up her chilled hand and held it firmly in his grip. She tried to shy away from him and Cole sensed a war going on inside her, but he wouldn't let her untangle her fingers. The pad of his thumb rubbed a circle on the back of her hand as he tried to infuse a bit of warmth into her.

"But how —" Cole answered the question himself. While Sally Bancroft had been a loving, giving person, her husband, Charles, could frighten a charging black bear with a look. The daughter had run away a few years before Cole was born. Obviously, she'd kept her own daughter's birth a secret. "I'm sorry, Abby."

The grandfather clock in the corner

chimed ten times. The day slipped away, yet Cole didn't have the energy to move as he sat next to Abby and watched the sunlight spill in through the stained-glass portion of the windows and dye the room with multiple colors. Peace settled inside him and he sensed a new beginning. It wouldn't be easy, nothing worthwhile in life ever was, but the Lord would see him through and steer him in the right direction once his obligations were fulfilled.

"It's not your fault." Abby pulled away from Cole, not understanding why she suddenly wanted to rest her head on his shoulder. "Who knows what we'll discover while we're fixing this place up. Someday you'll have to tell me about them but not now. Too much to do."

And that "too much to do" didn't involve sitting next to Cole, being lulled into a sense of companionship and trying to figure out why she should keep her distance.

"I agree." Cole stood and held out his hand to help Abby to her feet.

Another shift of energy passed between them, leaving her out of breath and out of sorts. Fortunately, the tremors in her heart didn't show in her voice. "Come on. Let me show you the rest."

Hours later Abby and Cole sat back down

at her kitchen table, a legal-sized pad of paper between them. "You're in luck, Abby. From what I can see, this place is structurally sound, and aside from some water damage to the front and side porches, the work is all cosmetic. There may be problems we can't see though."

The timer dinged from the coffeemaker as Cole drew bold slashes across the first yellow page. Abby refilled their cups and returned to the table before he flipped it over and started drawing on the next sheet. By the fifth page, Abby's curiosity increased. With his head bent slightly to his left, she could see the tip of his tongue protruding from his lips as he worked. Strong, firm fingers wrapped around the pencil, and from Abby's earlier experience, she knew they were rough from hard work, yet gentle when he'd held her hand in the living room.

The almost schoolboyish image he portrayed when he shoved the pencil behind his ear, and the excitement dancing in his eyes when he gazed up at her, made breathing more difficult. She definitely should have never let him into the house.

"Okay, Abby, here's what I think needs to be done." Cole shifted the pad across to her and then stood to reposition his chair around the table next to her. His nearness threatened her sanity again. Instinctively, she shied away even though she never moved her seat. "We need to get rid of all the wallpaper, the paneling and carpet and see how bad it is underneath. All the wood needs to be stripped of the paint and re-stained its original color. The walls can either be repainted or wallpapered. There should be original pictures that we can refer to somewhere in the town archives if there aren't any here. That would also give us a sense of the furniture, too."

More excitement laced his voice as he flipped over the first page. "The main floor should be our initial focus because that's what people see first. The living room needs to be warm and inviting so your guests can unwind and relax after a long day. The French double doors can close and separate the parlor from the reception area, which could double as a temporary office for those who need to work, and you could offer Wi-Fi services for those who can't live without internet for a few days. The dining room might be a little small depending on the number of guests, but in the summer months, they could sit out on the front veranda and enjoy the views and the weather."

All Abby saw in his scribbled notes was

sand sifting quickly through an hourglass. Her stomach clenched. What the man outlined would take way more time and money than she'd budgeted for and she hadn't even started to furnish or decorate the place yet. She should have known this wasn't going to be easy. Nothing in life ever was. Yet, selling wasn't an option because she was determined to stick it out and put down roots so she could find an inner peace that had eluded her for her entire life.

"When does your crew arrive? Are you sure we can do all this in two months? How much money?" Abby had better get a time frame and a figure before she trudged to apply for a bank loan. Her fingernails dug into her palms, tamping down his enthusiasm before it could wear off on her.

"I don't have a crew anymore." Cole squeezed the bridge of his nose and his shoulders slumped.

Ragged breathing forced air into her lungs. Obviously Abby wasn't the only one with past issues. A piece of hopelessness fell away and she fought the longing to comfort Cole as he had done for her.

Cole's strained sigh filled the gap between them. "I'll get it done. As for money, we'll figure out what we'll need in materials when you tell me what you want. Fortunately, your grandparents already added more bathrooms upstairs and converted the servant's hallway into a powder room, but they need to be redone along with everything else in this house. You'll also have to decide whether you want to convert the space in the attic into living quarters or take the room your grandparents used, and how big of a kitchen you think you'll need. I'd suggest taking the butler pantry and enlarging the entire room, but that's your choice."

Everything Cole said spun around in Abby's mind like a top. Her fingers tightened on the edge of the table and she squeezed her eyelids shut, blocking out his drawings and scribbled notes.

"Abby?" His voice filled her ears, his warm breath tickling her lobe. "Are you okay?"

"I'm fine." Her heart wedged in her throat when she opened her eyes and turned to stare into his. The hammering in her brain intensified and swallowing became a chore.

The trill of the phone shattered the invisible thread binding them together. After scraping her chair's legs against the linoleum floor, she lunged for the phone hanging on the wall next to the outdated refrigerator. At least this one was a little more current than the one in the office. "Hello? I mean,

Bancroft Bed-and-Breakfast, Abby speaking. How may I help you?"

Abby listened to the voice on the other end. She stared at Cole, who still sat scribbling more notes on the paper, a slight frown hugging his lips. White knuckles protruded from his long, lean fingers as he squeezed the pencil. His actions contradicted his earlier words. "You'd like to book a room?"

Cole's eyebrows rose, his brown eyes piercing her.

"Of course we do." Turning away from the contractor, Abby found a piece of paper and wrote down all the necessary information to transfer to the ledger later. "Thanks, Mrs. Andrews. We'll see you at the beginning of May."

Lifting her chin, Abby twirled around and leveled her gaze on Cole again. Determination filled her. She was her mother's daughter after all and until the end, nothing could stop Sharon Bancroft when she set her mind to something. "Great. Another reservation. I sense some conflict in you, Mr. Preston. I'm here for the long haul. I have to make this work. We have two months to pull this place together. If you don't feel you're up to the task, then leave. I won't hold it against you."

A dog barked from the neighbor's yard, breaking the uncomfortable silence.

"The name's Cole. And I'm more than capable of the task."

She hated pushing Cole, but she needed to know where he really stood. Her voice softened. "Fine. Then we'd better get started, hadn't we? We can begin on the main floor and do the bedrooms as we need them. Right now I have two reservations, so that leaves four rooms we can work on later unless I book more guests."

A knock at Abby's front door caught their attention.

With the frown still hugging his lips, Cole set down the pen on the paper and stood. "Sounds doable. Are you expecting any-one?"

"No." Abby pushed away from the counter, glad for the distraction as she headed for the sound. "It must be Mrs. Wendt again. She's probably brought me something else to eat. She thinks I'm too skinny."

Cole intercepted her, his gaze traveled slowly from the tips of her sneakers to the bandanna on her head. When his fingers tenderly brushed away a piece of dust from her hair, her breath caught in her throat and refused to move into her lungs. His appreciative glance finally settled on her face. "I think you look fine."

"Thank you. I think."

"You're welcome." He turned and strode from the room. "I'll get it."

"No. I'll get it. It's my house." A louder knock brought Abby out of her reverie. "Hang on, I'm coming."

Heat flared in her cheeks as she scurried down the hall and overtook Cole in the reception hall. He hovered behind her but allowed her to struggle with the lock, until she finally managed to jiggle the dead bolt and open the front door. An elderly woman stood on the porch, her hand patting down a stray flyaway from her salon coiffed hair, a nervous smile gracing her brightly painted lips.

"Hello, Ms. Bancroft, My name is Kitty. Kitty Carlton. I used to help your grandmother with the housekeeping. I'm here to offer my services to you when you reopen." The woman's high-pitched words strung out in one big breath.

"Hi, Kitty. It's a pleasure to meet you." Abby's lips pulled back, exposing her teeth, but a smile took a long time to form. She extended her hand to shake Kitty's limp one. The woman's clammy grasp reminded her of the worms she used to put on the hooks when she went fishing in the pond behind one of their many apartments in L.A. She did her best not to shake off the feeling when she let go or rub her hands across her jeans. Abby motioned for Cole to join her. "Thanks for your offer. I don't need anyone quite yet. Not until the beginning of May. Cole and I are just going over the remodeling that needs to be done before I reopen, aren't we, Cole?"

"Cole? Cole who? I'd heard that you came alone." Kitty's open curiosity stung at the privacy Abby guarded carefully. The less people knew about her personal life, the less likely they were to hurt her emotionally. A lesson she should learn with Cole, yet somehow she sensed, or maybe hoped, he'd be different.

Cole stepped out of the shadows. "Hello, Mrs. Carlton."

All the color fled from the elderly woman's face, her voice frigid with contempt. "You have some nerve showing your face in this town, Cole Preston."

Abby's stomach nose-dived to her feet. Between the handshake and her reaction to Cole, the woman wasn't making a good lasting impression on her. It was all she could do not to shut the door in Kitty's face, yet if she did, word would get around and probably ruin her chances of fitting in. Or would siding with Cole destroy it? Indecisions clawed at her until she knew what she had to do. "Why? He's come to do the work."

Kitty's piercing gaze stayed on Abby. "He's trouble, that one. A bad seed like his dad. *I* wouldn't let him inside my house or anywhere near my property."

The woman's remarks continued to upset Abby. No one deserved such rude treatment no matter what the circumstances. If anyone should hold a grudge, it should be Abby, and yet she couldn't find the way to do it. He had come to do the work after all, even if he was a year late. She lifted her chin and clenched her hands together. There was no way she'd ever hire Kitty Carlton to do one lick of work inside her home without a huge attitude adjustment. "Thanks for stopping by. When Cole and I are done with the remodel, I'll let you know if I need your services."

"Why, after what happened and how he killed your grandparents —"

"Now, now, Kitty. You know that's not true. Charles had a bad heart and Sally couldn't go on without him." Mrs. Wendt tsked as she climbed up the front steps with a plate of fresh baked cookies in her hand. The aroma of oatmeal and cinnamon drifted by Abby's nose, carried in on a small gust of cold air. "Besides, if I remember correctly, it was his partner that took the money. Why don't you go bother someone else with your lies and sour attitude and leave these two alone?"

Abby could have hugged her neighbor as the other woman retreated down the steps. "Goodbye then."

"Good riddance is more like it. Maybe if she found the Lord, she'd be more forgiving and accepting. Hi, Abby. Cole. It is good to see you again. It's time you came home." The older woman raised her eyebrows and stepped past him. Once inside the foyer, she glanced around. "My, my, this place does need some work, doesn't it?"

"Hi, Mrs. Wendt. Yes. Abby and I were just going through what needs to be done." Cole wedged a hand through his hair and stepped back. His gaze met Abby's.

"Why, that's wonderful. That means you'll be here for a while." Speculation sprinkled the elderly woman's expression. "Phillip will be tickled. You don't happen to have a son that can shovel our walk now, do you? Or rake our leaves or mow our lawn?"

"No. I'm not married."

"Not married? What a shame." Mrs. Wendt winked at Abby. "You'd be a fine catch for some lucky, single, young lady. Abby, I made you some cookies and came by to retrieve my casserole dish."

Cole's stiffening back didn't go unnoticed. Her neighbor's words made him uncomfortable; her, too. Abby wasn't here to find romance.

"How's your husband doing?" Cole questioned, as if trying to steer the conversation to a more neutral ground.

Abby released the breath she held and filled her lungs with much needed oxygen. Mrs. Wendt's gaze kept darting between the two of them and mischief crept into her smile. Dread filled Abby. Cole had admitted earlier he wasn't the stay-around-for-the-long-haul kind of guy.

"Just fine, though his arthritis is acting up with the cold weather. He wants to move but I can't imagine leaving Dynamite Creek for Phoenix. This is my home and where I'm needed. So, Cole. Where are you staying while you do the restorations?" All innocence fled the woman's expression and Abby's knees threatened to have a meeting with the thin rug under her feet.

Abby watched Cole back up until the railing stopped him. "I haven't given that much thought, Mrs. Wendt. My first priority was to come here and get started on the house."

"Well, I know it's not much, but Phillip and I have a small apartment above the garage that we've been wanting to rent out for a while. That way you won't have a long commute to work." Determination gleamed in her eyes. The woman's grin released a million butterflies in Abby's stomach.

It took a few seconds for Cole to formulate an answer that Abby suspected was more for her benefit than Mrs. Wendt's. "That's very kind of you and it would be convenient. I haven't had a chance to speak to my sister, but I suspect her place probably isn't big enough for a semi-temporary guest and my mother's is out of the question." Cole's gaze flipped between the two. "As long as you understand it's nothing permanent. I'll be moving on when I'm done here."

Relief and disappointment filled Abby, yet she schooled her expression to remain neutral. It was nothing she hadn't expected anyway.

"I understand completely. I'll go put fresh linens on the bed and find the extra key. Oh, and I have a coupon for Mama Zita's. It's the best pizza in town, you know. Phillip can't have it because of his high cholesterol, but you just have to try it tonight. Neither one of you had any dinner plans, did you? No? Good. I'm sure you'll still have lots to discuss for what needs to be done here." Helen thrust the plate of cookies into Abby's hands and hummed on her way out the door.

Abby's jaw dropped and the butterflies inside her refused to be stilled. With Cole living next door during the restorations, she'd find no peace of mind at all. Especially when his new landlady appeared to have matchmaking on her mind.

CHAPTER THREE

The knock on her front door just before seven o'clock still took Abby by surprise even though she expected it. Agreeing to Helen Wendt's scheme of sharing a pizza at home with Cole so they could continue to go through plans probably wasn't one of her smartest moves. Not like she had much choice in the matter. Her fingers smoothed out a tiny crease in the blue and white floral printed tablecloth she'd found in the linen closet. The automatic gesture reassured her, reminding her of how she used to rub her blankie between her fingers to calm down when she was a child. She glanced around the dining room before she stepped into the reception area.

Her low heels clicked against the wood flooring and now she questioned her sanity as to why she'd changed into a skirt. Or let her hair down. Or applied just a hint of makeup. Would Cole think that she was going to be a willing participant in Mrs. Wendt's matchmaking scheme?

Her nervous sigh rattled all the way to her toes. Too late to change now.

Light spilled in through the stained-glass window and beyond the pane Abby could see Cole's silhouette against the dark backdrop. Distorted and colorful, yet tied together into a recognizable shape, his image reminded her of a Picasso she'd studied in art class.

She took a deep breath, flipped her hair behind her shoulders, and then rubbed her damp hands over the black skirt. The lock didn't want to slide back again, which didn't help her nerves. Finally, using her shoulder, she pushed against the door to relieve some of the pressure on the lock and tried again. This time it worked.

Pulling back the oak door, she saw Cole balancing a large square box with a white plastic bag set on top. His hesitant smile signaled that, like herself, maybe he wasn't as comfortable with the dinner idea, either. "Hi, again."

"Hi, yourself." Abby took the box and watched as Cole carefully wiped his feet on the mat before he shrugged out of his black jacket and hung it on a hook on the hall tree.

He retrieved the pizza. "Thanks."

"We're in the dining room tonight. I thought it would give us more room."

"Good idea." When he moved passed her, the hint of freshly applied aftershave drifted by her nose. His still slightly damp hair curled away from his forehead. Abby forced her hand to remain at her side instead of reaching out to touch it. This reaction to Cole was crazy. He was her contractor. Nothing more.

"Smells delicious." Abby took her own seat kitty-corner from where Cole stood and settled the blue linen napkin onto her lap.

"It is." Cole opened the plastic bag and pulled out a baggie full of celery, some Ranch dressing and a Styrofoam container and placed them on the table. "I also took the liberty of getting some barbecue chicken wings. Mama Zita's place *is* the best in town. Or it used to be anyway."

Then he flipped up the lid to the cardboard box, revealing the thin crust pie covered in pepperoni, sausage, onions, green peppers and olives. The tangy aroma teased her taste buds and made her mouth water. Her stomach growled in anticipation because she hadn't eaten anything since a peanut butter and jelly sandwich at noon.

"Wow. It looks wonderful, Cole." Abby

held up her delicate china plate so Cole could set the slice of pizza on it.

His eyebrows lifted. "Plates? I'm sure I could have gotten some paper ones at Mama Zita's."

Abby set it in front of her. "I found paper plates in the pantry. I didn't want to use them."

"Why not? They're so much easier to clean up." A frown emerged as his gaze roved over her face as if he were trying to make up his mind about her.

She could almost hear the imaginary taunts she'd thought she'd left behind in her awkward teenage years. She knew it had been silly of her to use the plates in the large, built-in cabinet behind her but Abby dared to hope Cole would understand her odd behavior. Her pointer finger traced the gold edge of the antique ivory plate with the multicolored floral print painted on the surface.

"Paper means temporary and on the move and seems a bit impersonal. I want permanence. They're not exactly my type but they fit with the theme I envision for the house."

"There's nothing wrong with that. It just surprised me. Outside of a restaurant, I haven't eaten off a real plate in years." Cole tucked his napkin on his lap, a hesitant smile creeping across his lips. His confession only solidified his lack of willingness to stay in one place. "You and my sister would get along. She refuses to use paper or plastic because it brings up painful memories."

"Oh. I'd like to meet her sometime."

"I'm sure you will. Christine lives on the other side of town but she owns a cute boutique on Main Street. She makes candles for a living."

Pleasure filled her, yet panic tried to take hold. Cole noticed. Abby bit her lip and glanced away from the twinkle in his eyes. She may have gone overboard though with the candle in the slightly tarnished pewter candelabra gracing the center of the table. The dancing flame created an almost intimate and romantic atmosphere, virtually blocking out everything but the two of them. She grabbed her crystal goblet and drank most of the water inside. While it quenched her parched throat, it didn't come near to satisfying her need to fit in.

But her lopsided attraction wasn't the only thing that made her squirm when she picked up her slice. After Cole helped himself to his own pizza and wings, he folded his hands together and bowed his head. Heat creeping to her cheeks, she quickly set down her food and mimicked

Cole's movements. At least he hadn't asked her to say the prayer.

"Dear Lord, bless this food and this house. May the restoration go quickly and easily. Amen."

"Amen." Abby found herself saying the word. She didn't choke, nor did any lightning bolts appear from the sky. Having heard it many times, she discovered it wasn't as foreign to her as she'd thought. Abby had just never felt the urge to say it before tonight. Maybe she should go through more carefully the packet Delia gave her and explore the possibilities of religion when they finished the house. If she could open her practical mind and believe . . . Right.

If God truly existed, why did He let such bad things happen around the world? Why did He take her mom?

Abby picked up her slice again and bit into the pizza. As anticipated, the varied toppings exploded across her taste buds. "This is wonderful. I've never had such a combination before."

"Really?" Cole rested his arms against the side of the table and searched her face. "I thought it was pretty standard. I would have gotten mushrooms, too, but I wasn't sure if you'd like them."

"I do, actually." Abby fell into his warm and inviting gaze. A hint of a smile tugged at his lips and the flame's reflection danced in his brown eyes. The combination of the candlelight, the inviting scent of pizza and the light sound of classic rock music from the old radio she'd found in the kitchen loosened her tongue. "But a lot of toppings are expensive. When my mom could afford to buy a pizza, we only got cheese. And that wasn't often."

Cole's expression shifted in the flickering light. "I'll remember that next time. Things changed in my family, too, when my parents split up. Going out to eat, taking in a movie, or even getting the bare necessities like winter gloves and a scarf was a challenge."

"So that's why you shoveled my grandparent's walkway." Abby gladly shifted the conversation back to Cole. She didn't want to dwell on the next time or the idea that they had anything similar in their backgrounds because that would probably make her like him more than she already unwillingly did. "And probably why you moved to Phoenix."

"Among other reasons. I couldn't wait to get out of this place."

Abby's heart stalled at his words. All her life she'd wanted to stay in one place for more than six months. To have what her temporary classmates had. To belong and have a place to call home. She couldn't imagine wanting to leave Dynamite Creek, and now that she'd found it, she would do everything in her power to be able to stay.

She chewed another mouthful of pizza, realizing she knew nothing about the man next to her except he was about her age and a contractor. If they were to work together, having more background information could only be helpful. Right. She forced herself to swallow, knowing her interest was more personal than professional. "How old were you when you left?"

"Nineteen." A frown twisted his features as he placed another slice on her plate.

Unused to being served, his action addled her brain. The gentle way he scooped up the wayward bit of sausage and set it back in its place sent her pulse fluttering. If he treated her house that way, or even herself, Abby would have a hard time not falling for him and the way he seemed to care for everything around him. "Thanks."

His gaze captured hers and Abby couldn't pull herself from the depths of uncertainty or the hint of despair. Instinctively she leaned closer, wishing she could erase the haggard lines creasing his face, but to do so would be crossing the barrier she'd erected to keep people at a distance.

"I may as well tell you the truth before someone else does. I made some bad choices and got into some trouble here. Vandalism. A prank gone bad. One of my old neighbors intervened with the judge and hooked me up with his brother who owned a construction firm in Phoenix. I liked what I was doing and enrolled in trade school. A few years after I graduated, I struck out on my own."

"Interesting." Abby leaned back, any lingering intimacy shattered by Cole's revelation. Not good. It reminded her of her mother and why they'd had to keep moving. Her head buzzed and her appetite disappeared. Trouble seemed to follow him. Or maybe he actively sought it out?

She should release him from his obligation, but then she'd never get the house done on time or anywhere close to the beginning of May. Would her association with him help or hurt her chances of fitting in? Judging from the few people she'd met, it could go either way, yet she didn't have the heart to turn him away because she couldn't reconcile the man sitting next to her with what his partner had done or the poor decisions he'd made in his youth. His actions spoke differently, which was why she needed to give him a chance.

Their conversation turned back to the house as she forced herself to eat the last slice of pizza. At the end though, she still struggled with her curiosity. "What made you decide to do restoration work instead of new construction?"

The clink of ice shared the space between them as Cole lifted his goblet to his lips and drank. Abby couldn't stop staring at the strong column of his neck or the way his Adam's apple bobbed as he emptied the glass. Finally her glance shifted to the cleanly shaven skin covering his angular jawline and then upward to his firm lips. She wondered how they would feel against hers.

Her breath hitched. The atmosphere in the house only added to her confusion. Going along with Helen's scheme and eating dinner with Cole had been a bad idea, especially since she couldn't think of the last time she'd shared a meal with anyone other than lunch with one of her ex coworkers. Yet he sat at the head of the table like he belonged there. As if this space which had been built over 135 years earlier had been constructed with him in mind. He fit into her house, but from what she'd discovered, would never fit into her life. She had to remember that so she wouldn't get hurt again.

Cole placed his goblet on the table and stared at it intently. His finger traced the intricate pattern cut into the crystal. "Look around you, Abby. This place is a work of art. Unlike the boxes being built today, it has character and life. I'm the artist, dedicated to bringing back the vision that the original builders had in mind. Nothing more. Nothing less. I built my reputation on that and I think that's why your grandparents hired my company. They wanted to leave you a legacy."

Her fingers mangled the pizza crust. "I doubt it. As far as I know, they didn't even try to look for my mom or me. It would have been nice to know I had more family somewhere."

Cole removed the remains from her hands and wiped her fingertips gently with his napkin. His actions made her dizzy and breathing a chore, yet she didn't want the moment to end. "There's always two sides to every story. Maybe someday you'll discover them. Until then, let's keep moving forward on the house."

The house. Good idea. Focus on what's important. Not the niggling notion that maybe things weren't quite what they seemed.

Releasing her hand, he pushed the plates to the side. Abby knew it was for the best and willed her heart to quit its frantic beating. She inhaled sharply, forcing her attention from the man to the candle gracing the center of the table and blew out the candle. A puff of smoke wafted between them, temporarily breaking the spell.

"Good idea." Her voice shook despite her attempt to act normal.

She grabbed for the pizza box the same time Cole scooped up the Styrofoam container. Stunned, Abby watched him wedge the container of Ranch dressing inside with the remaining chicken wings, dump the bones from one china plate to the other, and then stack the plates on top of each other. Cole must have seen her mouth drop open even though she tried to cover it with a yawn.

Shrugging, his lips twisted into a half grin. "What? I was raised to do my share."

Her mother had obviously been hanging out with the wrong men during Abby's childhood. Abby followed Cole into the kitchen, taking in the breadth of his shoulders underneath his pale blue collared shirt. She hadn't paid attention earlier. She sure did now. Her mouth went dry. Somehow she managed to place the leftover pizza in the box on the counter but not before their shoulders grazed. The instant surge of awareness kicked her heartbeat into another rhythm. Heat colored Abby's cheeks.

"Where did you put the garbage can?" Cole stepped to the side and held up the plate with the chicken bones.

The not-so-spacious area seemed to grow smaller the longer he remained. "Under the sink."

Instead of looking at Cole, or more specifically the light sprinkling of hair on his long, lean fingers, as they held the plates, Abby stared at the kitchen with new eyes. The room would be the last place she fixed up because guests wouldn't be allowed inside, but it would be nice to have new amenities like a dishwasher and a refrigerator with an ice and water dispenser. All luxuries she'd grown up without and cost money she didn't have. A new stove would be a good idea, too, if she could figure out how to use one to do more than the basic stuff.

Abby shook her head to dispel the images of fires and other cooking disasters. She had to learn how to make blueberry scones and other tasty treats to tempt her guests and make them happy. She'd promised her first customers. Of course, to begin with, she had to find the recipe.

"This will just take a moment. I'll meet you back in the dining room when I'm done."

Cole searched her expression as he put the two dishes in the sink and finally left the room, giving Abby a moment to breathe before putting the leftovers away. Turning on the hot water faucet, she washed the plates and wished she could wash away his imprint as easily as she did the crumbs.

Disappointment and exhaustion filled her. Turning on the tap again to rinse off the dishes, Abby watched the water spill over her hands and shoot out in different directions. Unlike her emotions, the water represented a release she dared not show. He was just like everyone else in her clichéd life. Here today, gone tomorrow. Cole was simply her contractor, not a prince in one of the fairy tales her mother used to read her. She'd best remember that before she made a fool of herself.

The sound of footsteps interrupted her thoughts. Her spine stiffened, and she shut off the tap before reaching for the dish towel on the counter. She spied Cole's reflection in the window above the sink as he stood in the doorway and strangled the towel she'd picked up to dry her hands.

"Abby, I want to show you something."

"No problem. I'll be right there."

When Abby finally returned to the dining room a minute later, Cole stood on one of the wooden chairs. Balancing his weight on the edges, he lifted his hands to the ceiling and knocked on the drywall. Hollow, just as he thought it would be.

"What are you doing?" Abby stared at him perplexed.

"I'm testing the ceiling." Cole jumped down and walked over to her, wanting to erase the faint lines creasing her expression. "This is a drop ceiling. See how much lower it is than the rest of the ceilings in the house? I should have noticed it earlier, but unlike the other rooms, I didn't spend much time in here until dinner. Sometime in the past, someone put this up."

"Why would they do that?" Abby shook her head and crossed her arms in front of her as if she couldn't figure out what to do with them.

After motioning her to sit down, Cole inhaled sharply when he sat down on the chair he'd just used as a stool. "There could be any number of reasons, but the most probable one is water damage to the plaster underneath and this was the cheapest way to fix it. Look at the light fixture. It doesn't match the rest in the house."

"You're right. It doesn't match and it's ugly." With a sigh, Abby rested her elbows on the table and started to curl a section of her hair around her right finger. "How will you be able to tell?"

Her unspoken vulnerability gnawed at his confidence. Despite the coolness inside the house, sweat gathered underneath his arms and on his forehead. "I'll have to pull down one of the tiles and look inside unless you want to leave it as is."

Abby stood, her chair scraping across the wood floor. Cole winced at the sound and at the fleeting tide of panic spreading across her face. He suspected they both knew what would be underneath the false ceiling when he took a look tomorrow morning.

He followed her as she marched to the reception area, to the living room and then back to the dining room. She whirled around to face him and her green eyes reminded him of a new blade of grass on a spring day, filled with promise and yet still unsure of the future. Her fingers played with the tips of her hair again, this time accompanied by her teeth worrying themselves into her bottom lip. "And if you find water damage, what then?"

"Then we fix it." Cole wished he felt as

confident as his voice sounded. What if he were mistaken again? But in this instance it would be a good thing if Abby's grandparents had simply wanted a dropped ceiling. His gut churned and if he listened to what it was saying, the damage would be far worse than he imagined. If he could trust what he was trying to tell himself.

"Fixing it will take more money and more time."

"I'm afraid so. Let's hope it's nothing serious."

Unable to keep up the brave front before Cole, Abby turned her back on him and stared at the ceiling again, even more overwhelmed than before. More problems. More delays. The weight of the work needing to be done pressed down and suffocated her until she could scarcely fill her lungs. What else could go wrong?

Tears pooled in her eyes and threatened to spill over. Panic flared inside her. Crying never solved anything. It only brought ridicule to the new eight-year-old kid on the playground. Since that day, Abby had only broken down once and that was at her mother's funeral. She wouldn't let Cole see her moment of weakness.

Keeping her back to him, Abby leaned forward and picked up her napkin. Refolding it into a square, she placed it again on the table and then did the same with the one Cole had used. As she stared at a crumb that had fallen off one of the plates, she managed to remove the tremor from her voice. Yes, she was running away from her problem, but it was the only thing she knew how to do right now. "You know, Cole, thanks for bringing the pizza and wings, but I'm really tired. The long drive from L.A yesterday and getting up early this morning and everything. I know we have a lot more to discuss, but it has to wait until tomorrow."

Abby heard the house creak in the stillness between them. Awareness singed her being as Cole moved in behind her, his breath tickling the top of her head. She envisioned his arms around her and even sensed him reaching out to her, until she heard the telltale sign of his arm dropping to his side. The warmth of his sigh caressed her until he backed away. She wanted him to stay.

"That sounds like a plan. I'm tired myself. I'll let myself out. See you in the morning. Please make sure to lock up after I leave." Floorboards squeaked when Cole shifted his weight, the sound of retreating footsteps followed.

Just like that, he was gone. Sure, he'd be back tomorrow, but in two months' time, she'd be alone again.

Still a little mystified at Abby's odd behavior at the end of last night, Cole stood on her front porch at eight o'clock the next morning, ready to work. If she hadn't changed her mind. He'd seen the tears in her eyes. Why had Abby been about to cry? It couldn't have been something he said, could it? Their conversation rolled through his mind, but nothing out of the ordinary stuck out.

In fact, everything had been fine earlier. So what was it? And why did Cole want to know? He was better off not knowing. Not getting involved again. Yet his troubled heart refused to listen to the wiser voice in his head. He'd been down this road before with disastrous results, but somehow with Abby, he couldn't ignore it, although he knew now wasn't the time to bring it up.

Cold air danced across his exposed face. Freezing outside wasn't going to get anything accomplished while he wrestled with his conscience. He raised his hand to knock on the wood door, while in the other hand he carried a plate of fresh baked banana bread courtesy of his temporary landlady.

The door swung open on noisy hinges. Abby must have been waiting for him.

Or not.

Once he shifted his gaze past her startled face, he realized she wore running clothes underneath her jacket. With her hair pulled back into a ponytail and no makeup, she looked younger than the mid-to-late-twenties he suspected she was. Fuzzy muffs covered her ears; the teddy bear faces winked back at him. He smiled. Leave it to Abby to cheer up this gray, cloudy day with a chance of snow in the forecast. "Morning."

"Oh, Cole. Good morning. You startled me. I wasn't expecting you 'til nine. I really need to pay better attention." Abby's laughter came out in short gasps, crystallizing in the air between them. Her gloved hand stilled over her heart, yet an impish grin settled on her lips. "Do you always make it a habit to scare people?"

"No. Sorry, Abby. I had no idea you were literally on the other side. I guess setting up a time schedule for doing the work needs to be discussed, too. I like to start early." But Cole suspected Abby wouldn't want him banging around at 7:00 a.m. He ran his free hand through his hair and offered up the plate. "Here. Helen made this for you."

"How thoughtful. Thanks for bringing it over. Please put the plate on the kitchen counter and help yourself to some coffee if you'd like. I'm going for a jog. I won't be long." She looked longingly outside over his shoulder.

Cole had the urge to join her even though he wasn't dressed properly. From behind her, the tantalizing smell of brewed coffee and the warmth of inside beckoned. "Then I won't keep you. I'll start making a list of supplies for the basic things we discussed yesterday and take a look at the dining room ceiling."

With a nod, she slipped past him, flashing him another smile, and then was gone. Stepping inside the threshold, Cole pivoted around and stared at her retreating figure jogging down the street. Bad idea. He had a job to do. He'd better focus on that instead of Abby's shapely legs underneath her workout pants and bulky sweatshirt. The idea of another cup of coffee and the need to work on the interior finally won over his curiosity after she disappeared from view.

One cup of coffee and two slices of banana bread later, Cole surveyed the living room. In the gray light trickling in the windows, the room looked worse than it did yesterday. Dingy and cramped with its off-white painted walls, eclectic furniture and awful shag carpeting, the room needed more than a makeover to bring it back to its once stately fashion. It also needed a good dose of tender loving care to dispel the sad vibes lingering in the still air.

The parlor remained in bad shape, as was the hastily made office that once was part of the living room, too. Fortunately, the bedrooms upstairs only needed a fresh coat of paint or wallpaper and another layer of varnish on the surprisingly well-cared-for oak floors. The few imperfections could be covered with strategically placed rugs once Abby changed out or recovered the existing furniture.

The drop ceiling in the dining room concerned him, though. As he suspected, removing a tile confirmed his fears. He stuck his head into the hole and flashed a light into the dark interior. A musty odor filled his nostrils as dread weighed down on his shoulders. Extensive water damage. What plaster remained underneath was ruined. Replacing it would be nearly impossible. His ex-partner had been the master plasterer. They'd have to come up with another plan.

After dumping out the dregs of his coffee and rinsing the cup, Cole wandered back into the parlor, knelt down and began pulling up the shag carpeting. Where was Abby? He turned his head to look over his shoulder. The grandfather clock had chimed nine times fifteen minutes ago. Apprehension gnawed at his consciousness as he exposed the thin slats of wood beneath. His fingers ran over the worn, splintered surface. The entire floor in this room probably needed replacing, but it wasn't the work that bothered him. Abby had been gone over an hour.

Cole didn't jog; he preferred to work out in a gym, but he suspected it shouldn't take this long, especially in this weather. Releasing the carpet, he rose to his feet and strode to the side window. He pulled back the stiff lace, the now light gray lining and peered out the thin glass. A family of snowflakes drifted by and settled on a nearby bush.

Abby had headed east, but after this much time, Cole wouldn't have the first clue where to start looking even though he was familiar with the town. His fingers crushed the fabric, producing a small poof of dust that tickled his nose. He sneezed and then forced his muscles to relax. This was Dynamite Creek, not Phoenix or Los Angeles. Abby would be okay. But just in case, he sent up a quick prayer to the Lord to watch over her.

He'd seen her shift in her seat during his prayer at dinner last night and knew her discomfort. Cole figured she was in the same place he'd been a few long years ago, wandering alone and feeling displaced. Having found God, Cole was truly never by himself anymore and found relief in sharing his burdens, needs and hopes with His Father.

Even though he knew God had forgiven him for his share of his partner's indiscretions, he hadn't quite forgiven himself. Not until he'd finished his work here could he move on.

But if something happened to Abby . . .

The front door opened and quickly shut, but not before sending a blast of cold air into the house. Relief quelled his anxiety and in a moment he found himself standing next to her. Red colored her cheeks and the tip of her nose and a hitchhiking snowflake clung to one of her incredibly long eyelashes. A few tendrils of blond hair had escaped her ponytail and one of her earmuffs grinned back at him before she pulled it off with delicate fingers.

"Have a nice run?" Dumb question. Of course she had a nice run. Most people didn't do it unless they got some sort of enjoyment out of it but right now Cole was incapable of saying more. He wanted to voice his concern for Abby, but the words froze in his throat and refused to melt like the snowflake on her lashes. She'd probably mistake it for something else.

"Yes." She slid by him to hang her gloves and earmuffs on the coat rack to his left. "It was a little cold, but it's so peaceful and quiet around here and the air is so clean. So unlike L.A."

"Dynamite Creek does have its advantages." He flexed his fingers in order to keep from reaching to help her slip out of her zip-up sweatshirt. He suddenly didn't trust himself not to respond to the wave of vulnerability she unknowingly created.

"Sorry I took so long. I stopped to talk to another neighbor. Mr. Barrymore. He wanted to make sure I told you he said hello." Her glowing expression dimmed, yet she didn't elaborate on the conversation as she hung her sweatshirt on another hook.

Trepidation slammed him right between the shoulder blades. What had Mr. Barrymore said to Abby? Even though Cole had told her about the trouble, he hadn't elaborated in detail what he'd done. Her neighbor had been the one to bail Cole out all those years ago. Did his words have a double meaning or was Cole just being paranoid?

"I always respected him. I'll have to stop by and say hi when I get a chance."

At his response, a flicker of relief changed her eye color from cold glass to the jewel-colored seas of the Caribbean he'd only seen in pictures. "Did you make the budget? I need to see how much I can afford."

"Not yet. I've made more notes of what should be redone, but we're going to have to go to a few stores and check out a few online retailers to know the prices on some of this stuff."

"I should have internet service later today as soon as I put my computer back together. I have to warn you, though, I'm not crazy about shopping. I don't suppose you could do it without me?"

At her odd response, Cole knew there was another piece to the complicated riddle named Abby Bancroft. Every woman he knew loved to shop, yet somehow he knew Abby was different. He wondered if he'd be privileged to find out what deep emotions ran through her. Despite his decision to leave once he finished the job, he wanted to find out. "You don't like to shop? I thought that was a prerequisite for a woman?"

"Not this one." Abby's expression drifted somewhere into her past, and by the tension in her shoulders and the thinning of her lips he knew it wasn't a good memory.

He forced his arms to remain at his sides instead of wrapping them around her. "Care to tell me why?"

"You wouldn't understand."

Cole stepped forward until he stood inches from her. Then he tucked his forefinger under her chin and lifted her gaze to his. Something about this woman intrigued him to step out of his contractor mode. "Try me."

"It's no fun shopping when you can't afford anything but the castoffs from the rich kids you went to school with."

Despite her revelation, the story didn't quite match her earlier reaction. "That could be a problem, but I think there's more going on inside that head of yours right now."

A spark of anger flared before it fizzled into an emotional downward spiral. "Fine. I got lost among the racks of a discount store when I was four." Abby began to tremble, and suddenly Cole saw her as a scared child unable to find her mother. He gathered her in his arms and rested his chin on the top of her head. Her unique scent drifted under his nose, making it more difficult to remember he wasn't here to stay. "It was horrible. I couldn't find my mom. There were racks and racks of clothes and hangers, sleeves reaching out to grab me and fabric blocking my escape. Every way I went, there was only more clothing."

"I'm sorry, Abby. That must have been awful." Her warmth permeated his shirt and the realization that she felt right nestled in his arms concerned him enough to loosened his grip.

After a heartbeat, she pulled back and blinked, regaining her composure. "Enough about me. What's up with the dining room ceiling?"

All business again, Cole made sure not to add an optimistic quality to his voice. No use getting Abby's hopes up. "Are you ready to look at it?"

Her eyes clouded over. "It's ruined, isn't it?"

Cole fought the urge to comfort her as he broke the news. She wasn't his responsibility, and yet he cared enough to want to lessen her pain. "It's unsalvageable."

CHAPTER FOUR

"Unsalvageable? Does that mean I can't open by the beginning of May? I've taken reservations. And a deposit." Abby clenched her hands together, all the euphoria she'd gathered from running disappeared.

"No —"

"No as in no, I can't open or no, I can?" Abby marched past him and veered left when she got to the end of the reception room.

"No as in you can, but I'll have to work longer hours to get everything done."

"That's fine with me." But was it really? Could she handle him inside her house more than the time they'd already agreed upon? Once inside the dining room door-way, she paused and folded her arms across her chest. In the faded light filtering in through the lacy curtain, the room had lost its intimate glow from the candlelight, and the neatly folded napkins she'd left on the tablecloth last night looked lost and lonely. Abandoned. Story of her life.

Abby refused to feel sorry for herself. She had the power to change her future, starting with her house. This room. Adrenaline manifested in each pore again.

Behind her, Cole shifted his weight, and Abby sensed his uncertainty. If he couldn't do it, she'd do it herself. Her pride and reputation resided inside these walls and this dropped ceiling. There had to be a "How To" book in the local library or information somewhere on the Net. Determination propelled her across the scratched oak slats to the white tile propped up against the stepladder covered with a light dusting of powder. More powder covered the floor. Not a good sign, but instead of focusing on the results, she needed to see the problem. The opening in the ceiling was large enough to fit her head and arm into.

Cole followed closely behind her. His firm grip held the stepladder as she climbed to the second rung and popped her head inside. Darkness blinded her, yet the musty smell of stale air, worse than the odor already lingering inside the house, assaulted her nostrils. Even without seeing a thing, dread pummeled her insides and her hard-fought resolve faltered.

"Here. You're going to need this. It doesn't look like there's a mold issue, which will help tremendously." Cole clicked a button and pressed the flashlight into her open palm. As expected, a surge of energy passed between them that could have lit up the entire house. Too bad it couldn't magically fix all the problems and blemishes interfering with her tight timeline.

Abby lifted the light into the dark interior and worried her bottom lip as more panic blossomed inside her. A large section of the plaster had fallen away above her head, exposing slats of darkened wood and rusty nails. The beam of light picked up more damage at the back end of the dining room by the kitchen. Frustration glazed over her eyes when she spied what was left of an intricate mural painted on the upper wall. Time had been no friend to her inheritance.

Disappointed, Abby retracted the light, shifted her weight and lost her balance. The stepladder tottered and her right foot dangled in the air. Grabbing hold of the edge of the ceiling, she tried to right herself as Cole's arms wrapped around her legs. He steadied her, but both the flashlight and stepladder clattered to the floor, the loud bangs echoing in the room. A good size chunk of tile broke off in her hand causing more pieces of plaster dust to rain down on her head, the floor and table.

Dropping the tile, she reached for his broad shoulders, and her fingers enjoyed the wonderful play of his muscles as he gently let her slide to the floor. His grip moved to the curve of her waist while Abby struggled for breath.

Cole's brown eyes softened to creamy, rich, inviting chocolate. Time sped along, shifting her into another realm as she watched sunlight playfully create shadows on the planes of his face.

His hand drifted up slowly to brush away the dust from her cheek, the pads of his fingers lightly caressing her skin. Then his attention turned to removing whatever debris clung to her hair. "Are you okay?"

Abby nodded, her sneeze finally breaking the almost trancelike state between them.

She stepped away from him so she could think and found her voice. "I'm fine. Thanks for catching me. I wouldn't have been any use at all if I'd broken anything."

Moving to the old metal radiator to the left of the window, she hugged herself and stared at a patch of remaining snow nestled underneath a small pine tree. She could identify with the snow, struggling to find a welcome spot to hang on to. Eventually though, the sun and the change of season would chase away the safe haven. In Abby's case, she wouldn't become water and leach back into the ground, but disappear by getting back into her car and hightailing it out of town.

Would she still be here in a year? Yes.

A breeze picked up and a bare tree branch tapped against the rotting pillar by the small patio off the kitchen, yet she could imagine the possibilities. A nice row of red flowers hanging from the railing along with a rocking chair for those who craved tranquility. Newlyweds walking hand in hand as they strolled to the gazebo she planned to build next to the small pine tree. An elderly couple resting in the parlor after a long day of antique shopping.

The endless potentials excited her and for the first time, Abby would have a large part in making it happen. Unlike Cole, she was in this for the long haul. This time Abby was the tree and not the temporary snow. She could already feel her roots stretching toward the fertile ground. She was here to stay and that meant dealing with every blow that life decided to throw at her now.

The floor creaked as Cole righted the stepladder behind her and stooped to collect the flashlight that had rolled under the table. He clicked it on to see if it still worked. A beam of light reflected in the glass. Shutting out the image of the snow and concentrating on the tree, she turned around and faced Cole. "Okay, so the ceiling's ruined. How do we fix it?"

"You have two options." He rubbed his eyes before passing a hand across his face. His arm dropped to his side. "Three if you count keeping the dropped ceiling and just replacing the tiles." A hesitant grin settled on his lips.

Abby liked the way one corner of his mouth lifted and the way his dark hair caressed the worry lines on his forehead. She inhaled and took in his clean, fresh scent and felt his pull. Instinctively, she stepped back and repositioned her arms across her chest. "What are the first two?"

"Number one would be to replace the plaster. Number two is to replace the ceiling with drywall."

"Which would you suggest?"

"That's up to you. Redoing the plaster is not my specialty. It would take me at least three days or more and is costly but will retain the integrity of the house. Replacing with drywall will only take several hours, but will affect any resale value, depending on what the other homes in the area have done."

"What about the painting at the base of the ceiling?"

Cole yanked out a chair and straddled it, using the wood back as a chin rest. His fingers strangled the sides, causing his knuckles to whiten and clearly show through his skin. Shifting his gaze, he watched Abby pace back and forth, from the window to the hole above her head. The way she worried her bottom lip with her straight white teeth sent his need-to-fix radar into overdrive. He had to remind himself he was only responsible for the house and not the owner. He couldn't let any emotion cloud his vision. "If you choose the drywall option, it will be destroyed. If you choose the plaster method, it could be restored if you can find someone who can do it."

"What would you do?" Abby stopped pacing, and leveled her gaze on him.

The seat underneath him grew uncomfortable and Cole squirmed. Indecision twisted his gut. What would he do? He didn't know anymore. The choices he'd made in the past flitted through his consciousness. The mistakes. The misjudgments. Both options he'd just outlined had their own separate issues and drawbacks and he suspected if he chose one over the other, he'd be wrong. "I'll go with whatever you decide."

Abby sat down on the platform of the stepladder across from him and planted her chin on her fist. "That's a copout if I ever heard one."

"It's the only answer I have," Cole growled. Once his short, clipped words escaped his lips, he wanted to cram them back inside his mouth. Abby didn't need to be on the receiving side of his anger. He pinched the bridge of his nose and tried to ignore the hurt.

The drywall option suited Abby's time frame better, but he wanted to do the house right and redo the plaster. He owed it to Abby. Who needed sleep anyway? "Let's take down the drop ceiling so we can get a full assessment. I'll thoroughly check the rest of the house to make sure there's no other plaster damage and then we'll decide. Hopefully this is the only section that needs replacing although the paneling in the parlor concerns me."

"Sounds like a plan." Abby placed her hands on her knees and straightened her back.

Turning her head from side to side as she looked around the room gave Cole the perfect view of her long, elegant neck and the way her jaw jutted out in determination. He liked that in a woman. There were other things he liked about Abby, too, which scared him, like her confidence in him, their somewhat similar childhoods, and their love for the house.

He stood and pushed the chair back into position. "I'm going to run to the hardware store and get some prices on materials. I might go to Flagstaff if Lenny's doesn't have what we need."

"Okay. I'll set up my computer while you're gone."

Cole glanced at his watch, glad to escape the house and the feelings the woman inside evoked for a while. "Don't worry about lunch, I'll stop and pick something up on the way back."

In the office forty-five minutes later, Abby stretched her arms over her head and yawned. With her computer hooked up and the internet running, she could now start the tedious process of figuring out how to create a free website for the Bancroft Bed-and-Breakfast and a reservation system instead of the ledger way her grandparents had done it. She'd also need to put a marketing plan together if she had any hopes of getting a loan to cover some of the renovation.

"Meow." An animal's cry interrupted her and Abby jumped at the soft thud of something striking on the window. She glanced over to see a furry black cat with white paws balancing on the wooden frame. His big green eyes stared at her through the glass. A light wind ruffled his coat as his tail swished back and forth.

At first his presence frightened her, until a heartbeat later, Abby recognized another lost soul in the cat's unblinking stare. Was he just someone else looking for a home? Had he chosen this place for a reason? "Oh, you poor thing. Are you cold? Do you want in?"

Standing, she scurried to the kitchen and out the back door. "Here, kitty, kitty."

The cat bounded around the corner, leaped up the wooden stairs and padded across the porch. He butted his head against her jean-clad leg, arched his back and then rubbed his body along her calf. Abby's giggles filled the air as she reached down and stroked his fur, surprised to feel his backbone and ribs. Her laughter died. Maybe the cat had once belonged to her grandparents. Why else would he be so comfortable with his surroundings?

Abby scooped up the cat and cradled it to

her chest. Her fingers scratched underneath his chin, causing a rough purring sound. She'd always wanted a pet growing up, but her mother had told her pets didn't blend well with a transient lifestyle. Hope danced in her heart as she rested a cheek against his head. This was meant to be her home.

"Hello? Over here. Hi. I see you've met Cat," a voice called to Abby. Her hands tightened around the squirmy body and she tilted up her head to spy another elderly woman in a gray coat waving at her from the porch of the Victorian house on her right.

"Hello. The cat's name is Cat? That's strange. Did he belong to the Bancrofts?" Abby smiled as she watched the woman approach.

"I'm Betty Froehlich." Behind tortoise-shell glasses, curious yet welcoming blue eyes held hers. "No, he doesn't belong to anyone in particular. He's the neighborhood mooch. He comes and goes as he pleases, running from one house to another whenever it suits him. Your grandmother used to feed him, though. I suspect he thought Sally was back. God rest her soul."

Shifting her grip on the cat, Abby shook Mrs. Froehlich's hand. "Abby Bancroft. Pleased to meet you."

"No, Abby, the pleasure is mine. Wesley, that's my husband, told me not to bother you yet, but I just had to say hi when I saw you out and about. Here, this is for you. Blue Ribbon brownies. They're better than anything Helen Wendt can make. Even my banana bread is better. More moist." Betty practically shoved a covered dish into her hands before Abby could release Cat.

Overwhelmed again, Abby accepted the plate. She blinked. She'd only met some of her neighbors in L.A, much less have two of them thrust baked goods at her. Small town living proved to be more interesting. "Thanks, Mrs. Froehlich. That's very thoughtful of you."

"Please call me Betty. And you're welcome. It's what we Christians do, you know."

At another mention of God and religion, Abby shifted nervously. Was that all people in Dynamite Creek thought about?

"Oh, dear, I've made you uncomfortable now, haven't I? Don't pay any attention to me then. I talk too much." When the woman sidled around her and stepped to the back of the small area of the porch, Abby's gaze stayed on Mrs. Froehlich the entire time. Her neighbor's bony fingers reached out and stroked the pillar holding up the roof and she shook her head. "Such a tragedy. It makes me so sad."

"The Bancrofts or the house?"

"Both. I'm so sorry for your loss, Abby. Your family and this house used to be the talk of the town. And your mother . . . such a pretty thing. You look like her, you know. It was quite a shock to learn —" A blush graced the older woman's cheeks before she turned away. "Anyway, welcome to Dynamite Creek. We hope you like it here. I think I hear Wesley calling. Please let me know if you need anything. Anything at all. We're right next door, you know."

Abby nodded as her fingers tightened around the plate in her hands. She stared at Betty's retreating figure still unfamiliar with the open friendliness, so unlike the distant wariness she experienced in her tiny middle-class community in L.A. wedged between pockets of immigrants and poverty. Mrs. Froehlich's passing remark ticked her off. A shock to learn what? That the talk of the town now had an adult child? A child that grew up believing she had no family?

Funny how a law firm could find her in a matter of months, yet her grandparents could never be bothered to while they were alive. Abby's attention wandered to movement on the porch. Cat sat down and stared at her, his eyes unblinking before he started to lick his front paw.

The boards creaked under her feet as she spun to face the side yard. Sunlight spilled over the tops of the distant mountains and melted the snow clinging to the bare branches. Droplets of water sparkled like diamonds. The unfamiliar beauty astounded her and suddenly she knew things would work out. Abby held the back door open. "Come on inside, Cat. You're going to live with me now."

Cat made no move to step into the house. He sat on the porch expectantly waiting for something to fall from the plate, his tail swishing back and forth, and his ears alert. Moving across the wood planks, Abby knelt next to him and scratched him behind the ears. Another purr erupted. "Oh, no. These are for me. I'll run to the store and pick up some cat food for you. I get it now though, Cat. You're another wanderer like Cole. Kind of like I used to be. You know, settling in one place isn't so bad. Give it some thought."

Abby retreated into the house. Her gaze swept the porch again, but Cat had disappeared.

Stepping through the double glass doors of

Lenny's Hardware & Building Supply brought Cole back into a different decade. The place hadn't changed. The white tiled floors had cracked and dulled over time, but the ever-present smell of paint and varnish filled him with peace. Another layer of white covered the walls, making the metal racks and shelves stand out.

Merchandise filled every available slot and Lenny, now stooped with age, still sat behind the counter with his television on, which his old, faded eyes probably didn't even see anymore. Yet the man knew where everything was, how much of each he had and when someone was trying to outsmart him.

"Morning, Cole Preston. I was wondering when you'd show up here." Lenny Keefer's voice still rung with authority, which matched the wisdom etched into each wrinkle on his face.

"Good morning, Mr. Keefer. You knew it was only a matter of time." Cole walked up to the worn counter.

The white-haired man had been in his sixties when Cole's dad had first brought him here. Now eighteen years later, the man had obviously refused to slip into retirement like the other men his age, who kept the wood benches warm on the south side of the town square. Their whispers still echoed in Cole's ears.

"Heard you're working on the Bancroft Mansion." Lenny's gnarled fingers clutched the top of his cane, yet his light green eyes, washed out by time, held a twinkle.

Cole nodded, wondering what else the other man had heard. "Yes. That's why I'm here. To get some pricing for what I'm going to need."

A creaking noise interrupted the silence and Cole wasn't sure if it was the rickety old chair or Lenny's knees that made the sound when the man struggled to stand. "Things haven't changed much since you left, but let me show you around."

"That's all right. I know where everything is." Cole's words fell on deaf ears. The man inched around the corner of the checkout counter and headed for the rear of the store.

Following, Cole pulled out the small notebook from his back pocket and flipped it open. The slow pace gave him a chance to peruse the hardware shelves. His fingers remained still. Lots of brass, silver and gold knobs and hinges, but nothing that would match the broken and existing hardware in Abby's house without looking like an afterthought.

"The knobs you need aren't there. Those

107

are for those newfangled houses, not the Victorians." Lenny stopped and turned. He shook his head and motioned for Cole to keep up. "I might have what you want in the storeroom or one of the storage sheds out back."

Cole nodded and kept walking. His feet stopped outside the old workshop room to the right of the paint department. Memories slammed him in the gut and his fingers all but crumpled the notebook in his hand. His father brought him here a few times for the kids' building workshops on Saturday mornings. That had been the only time his dad had spent with him. When Will Preston wasn't too busy hitting the bottle or fighting with his wife. "You still do these?"

Lenny opened the door and switched on the light, illuminating three work tables with hammers and screwdrivers lined up on top. Small cans of varnish and paint along with various sizes of paintbrushes graced another table covered with old newspaper. "Of course. It's always been a big hit with the young 'uns."

Amid the underlying scent of varnish, Cole's fingers itched to rummage through the old box inside the small workroom in the back to pull out a project and put it together. He stepped inside and picked up a small wooden tool holder and ran his fingers over the smooth surface. The one he'd made had been lost over time with the numerous moves. Realistically, it was too small to be of practical use for him, yet it brought back the promise of a new future and what could be. It brought him to a happy place he wanted to find again. "I can see why. Those classes brought out my love of wood and working with my hands."

"I'm glad to see those workshops paid off for someone." Lenny leaned on his cane. "I've got a proposition for you."

Cole stilled and replaced the toolbox on the table. Tension gathered in his shoulders and across his temples. Those were the same words his ex-partner had used when Robert had approached him about joining forces all those years ago. "What is it?"

"The college kid I hired to do these workshops left a few weeks back because of his schedule. I've taken over in the interim, but quite frankly, these fingers aren't capable of doing it anymore." A look of disdain crumpled the man's features before his gaze pierced Cole's. "I need someone to take over or I'll have to cancel the workshops."

Lenny's words ripped a hole in Cole's heart. Those workshops had meant everything to him and he knew that somewhere in Dynamite Creek and in the outlying area, those workshops meant the world to another youth in desperate need to have something to believe in. Still he hesitated. He didn't think the old man had any motive other than what his words conveyed. Even four hours on a Saturday morning would make a huge impact in the time frame needed to get Abby's house done. "I'm only here temporarily, though."

"Be that as it may, I'll make it worth your while, Cole. I can't pay you more than minimum wage, but you'd get the employee discount on all the materials you buy. Twenty percent off could go a long way in fixing up the Bancroft Mansion." Mr. Keefer ushered him out of the room and back into the paint department. "Think about it while you're making your list and budget."

"Abby? I'm back." Cole slipped inside the house a little after one in the afternoon. Fatigue slowed him down and he hadn't even started the restorations yet. It would only get worse if he took the job at Lenny's but how could he let the workshop close and disappoint the kids? How could he disappoint Abby by not working on the house eighty hours a week? How could he

110

live with himself if he failed at both tasks?

White paper sack in hand because he'd stopped at the local burger joint, Cole nudged the front door closed with his foot, shutting out the cold. His footsteps echoed in the reception hall as he headed toward the kitchen. The house was eerily quiet, as if the massive Victorian held her breath, waiting. Waiting for what? To expose him for the fraud he felt like right now? Cole had seen the condemnation in old Mr. Wickham's eyes and heard his gruff voice as he'd stood in line waiting for his food. "Good-for-nothing, thieving, lying, worthless scum."

None of the other patrons, some he knew, most he didn't, had come to his defense. Not that he expected they would, but was he doing a disservice to Abby by coming here? He'd wash his hands of Dynamite Creek when he finished the house, but she would remain in a town where the prominent people had memories like elephants and were as unforgiving as the July sun in Phoenix.

His gaze scraped the interior of the kitchen. He had to fix this place up. He owed it to Abby.

"Abby? Are you here?" Placing the bag on the table, he yanked out a chair and dropped into the seat. No response. The kitchen was just as empty as the rest of the house. Good. Casting his exhaustion aside, he'd use the time to transfer the numbers from his small notebook to the large legal-sized pad of paper. After he ate, maybe Abby would have returned from wherever she'd gone so they could go online and look at things like the hardware and wallpaper. Cole pulled out the burgers and fries and lined them up on the table.

One for him, and one for Abby.

While his looked perfectly fine nestled in its wrappings, Abby's looked lost and out of place. He stood and retrieved one of the china plates she'd left in the drying rack and brought it back to the table. The plate reminded him of his temporary boss: delicate, feminine and permanent. He preferred plain, white and disposable.

Making sure the wrapper was tightly secured, he placed her food on the plate. Nothing he could do about the fries spilling across the surface but hope Abby came back soon.

After a quick prayer, Cole settled in his chair, unwrapped his burger and let the tantalizing scent fill his nose. Then he pulled out three of the ketchup packages, tore off the corner of the first and drizzled it onto the edge of the wrapper. No plate for him. Packets two and three followed until he had a satisfying pile for his fries, but even his actions couldn't eradicate the emptiness in the house. He missed Abby. His sigh filled the small space before he picked up his burger and opened his mouth.

The woman in his thoughts walked in through the back door with a grocery store bag in her hands. "Hi, Cole. Sorry I wasn't here. I had to run a quick errand."

"No problem. I just got here myself." Cole set down the burger and waited for Abby to join him. She'd showered since he'd left, and her fresh, herbal scent clung to her long, wavy locks that bounced around her shoulders. With her hair unbound, she looked like a different person as she emptied the contents of the bag. When she peeled off her jacket and hung it over the back of her chair, he noticed her dark green sweater magnified the color of her eyes and how her jeans fit her to perfection. But it wasn't just her physical appearance that attracted him. Squirming in his seat, Cole shifted his gaze to the counter. "Cat food?"

"There's a resident stray roaming the neighborhood. My grandmother used to feed him so I'm going to continue the tradition." Abby reached in the bag, grabbed a blue ceramic bowl and poured some of the dry kibble inside, then she set it outside the back door. "Here you go, Cat."

When she joined him, a blush flooded her cheeks as she noticed the plate underneath her lunch. She smiled, and Cole found himself on the receiving end of her happiness. He felt good.

For now.

He wanted to savor the moment, because once she saw his notes, her grin would evaporate faster than he suspected the cat food would in the dish on the back porch.

After they cleared the table, as Cole had predicted, her eyes widened when she saw his projections, yet inside their depths he saw her struggle for composure. What he'd proposed wasn't out of line, though he could scrimp and save in a few areas, or take the job that Lenny offered.

"But your partner — I saw the contract, his notes —"

"My *ex*-partner never had any intention of renovating this place." Cole clenched his fists but managed to keep them from banging on the table and upsetting Abby's water glass. He forced back the bile. "He was only interested in the money to relieve a gambling debt. Your grandparents weren't the only elderly clients he duped."

Cole fought for calm. He couldn't change the past or Robert's actions. He could only move forward and with the grace of God, make everything right. He was almost done. "The lies Robert promised were a little paint here and some over there. Like I told you before, this house needs a lot more to bring it back to its former glory. Please, just take a look."

He watched Abby stare at the numbers on the page. Her trembling fingers flipped through the drawings and lists and her teeth worried her bottom lip. Suddenly it was important to him to not only fix what was wrong with the house, but Abby, too. He wanted to bring back the sparkle he'd had a glimpse of after her earlier jog.

"I don't know, Cole. This is way more than I'd expected. I haven't even dealt with the furniture or accessories yet."

"I'm aware of that." Cole leaned back in his chair and clasped his hands behind his neck. "If you look at the last sheet, you'll see another set of numbers. I think those will make you feel better, but there's a catch."

Cole wished he were privileged to find out what went on inside her head as she stared at the last sheet. More worry lines creased her forehead and her gaze pierced his as she twisted a section of hair around her finger. "What's the catch?"

Cole struggled with his reply. "That's an employee discount if I work at Lenny's four hours every Saturday teaching a wood workshop for kids."

Abby's mouth dropped open and Cole heard her gasp for air. Color leached from her cheeks. "You'd do that to save me money?"

"Yes." Reaching over, he grabbed her hand and tried to infuse a bit of warmth back into her. His breath quickened when she didn't pull away. Holding her felt right, and wrong, and disoriented him. He watched her lips move in order to concentrate on her words.

"But how will you do everything? You need to sleep and eat and have some downtime. I can't let you do this. I won't let you." Her concern added a romantic quality to her voice and matched how he felt about this house and his new, yet temporary, boss.

"I want to. Don't worry about me. I'll get everything done and manage to survive." With regret he released her hand and stood. He had to get away before he decided moving on wasn't such a good thing after all.

CHAPTER FIVE

"We're here." At two-fifteen that afternoon Cole pulled his truck into an empty space recently vacated by a small, white SUV and parked the truck.

Sweat gathered on Abby's palms and her breathing barely filled her lungs. Outside her window, the two-story brick and stone building that took up a good portion of the block intimidated her with its row of arched windows and ornate architecture. Renaissance Revival popped into her head. Her early morning community college art history class had finally paid off. Her gaze quickly skimmed the large white-columned building situated in the center of the square, surrounded by mature trees. It reminded her of photos she'd seen of the Midwest.

Even the streetlight, a replica of the old Victorian globes, completed the picture. How quaint. Now all she needed was a horse-drawn carriage and a couple dressed in old-fashioned clothing to walk down the slightly newer sidewalk. The smell of diesel and a honking horn brought her back to the twenty-first century and to the building in front of her. "This is the Dynamite Creek National Bank?"

"What did you expect?"

Abby rubbed her hands across her floral skirt, glad she'd decided to dress for the occasion. "A regular looking branch, not something straight out of a classic movie."

Cole laughed and gave her a crooked smile as he opened the door and stepped out of his truck. He leaned back in for a moment. "Unless they've done some massive remodeling in the past two decades, wait until you see the inside. Hang on. Let me get your door. It sticks sometimes."

She watched him walk around the front of the vehicle, his stride powerful, his arms swinging by his sides. He opened her door, and her heart fluttered when he cupped her elbow and helped her down. Abby's last boyfriend had bought into the women's lib stuff and pretty much left her to fend for herself. Maybe breathing the air in this old-fashioned town brought out chivalry that seemed to be missing from the laid-back attitude of people where she'd come from. She found herself missing the beach, though the mountain air and the tall pine trees had begun to worm their way into her being.

Getting out of her seat, Abby sidestepped a woman holding the hand of a toddler and stared up at the building. Inside she imagined a bunch of stuffy, old men in gray suits sitting around a rectangular oak table, twirling their mustaches as wisps of smoke coiled up to the ceiling.

Maybe her skirt and a simple white blouse weren't enough. Maybe she should have worn a suit. All her possessions though, the ones she hadn't sold in the yard sale and couldn't fit into her car, including her simple navy blue suit, would arrive in a few measly boxes in the next couple days.

Her life in boxes, waiting to be released: a picture on the fireplace mantel, her collection of small glass figurines and a few treasured books from her childhood. Staying in one place for more than a year appealed to her. So did finally having the chance to become part of something. Anything. To finally belong somewhere even if she was the illegitimate grandchild.

Getting the bank loan would cement her place here. Sunlight stretched its warm embrace around her, blocking out her negative thoughts. Spring lay around the corner with a promise of a new beginning. She smelled it in the air and saw it in the ground with the few annuals poking their green stems through the dirt.

After Cole dumped a coin into the parking meter, her feet made short work of the cement and she craned her neck to look upward as they approached. She spied the date carved into the circle nestled inside one of the arches above the main entrance. *1901.*

"Built before Arizona became a state." Cole guided her up the steps, underneath a stone arch and then ushered her to the large revolving glass door. "After you."

"Thanks." Stepping inside the small area, she planted her hands on the metal bar and pushed. It wasn't as easy to move around as she'd thought and it wasn't until Cole got into the space behind her and pushed that the door began to spin. Careful not to let the rear glass panel clip her black heels, she stutter-stepped until she spilled into the cavernous interior.

She blinked after she pulled off her sunglasses. Abby had just stepped back in time. Apprehension gnawed at her confidence, even with Cole now at her side.

"Impressive, isn't it? Just as I remembered." Cole's voice poured over her like honey as he placed his hand on the small of her back. "The buildings here are what I missed most about this town. If we have time, I'll show you around the square."

"I'd like that." The contact heightened her senses on several levels and left her more out of sorts. She didn't know where to look first. Her gaze skittered from the black and white tile checkering the floor, to the heavy looking table stacked with deposit and withdrawal slips, to the wood barrier separating them from the bankers' desks.

"Welcome to the Dynamite Creek National Bank. I'm Tina, how may I help you?" A young, female teller greeted them from behind an ornate grill in front of her station.

His hand still on Abby's back, Cole escorted her to the teller window. To her left, a frosted panel of glass surrounded by more heavy dark wood hid the teller's computer screen. Up on the wall behind her, old paintings of the presidents gracing the American currency hung centered in the faux painted squares surrounded by hunter green vine. Patterned tin panels decorated the ceiling, while more modern fans hung down to circulate the air that smelled like money. Abby's stomach clenched again.

"Hi, Tina. We're here to see Stacy Moore if she's available."

"One moment please." The teller picked up the phone, another modern convenience that contradicted the aged atmosphere inside the bank. "Hi, Stacy. There's a couple here to see you."

Cole stiffened at Abby's side, yet he didn't contradict the woman.

"She'll be right with you." Tina smiled as she hung up the phone. "Please have a seat in the waiting area and help yourself to some coffee and cookies while she finishes up some paperwork."

"Thanks."

Abby's heels clicked on the tile as Cole led her to the small area nestled in the corner between the wood banister and the bank entrance. Four high-back brown leather chairs surrounded an antique table that had probably also been part of the original furniture. Beneath her feet, an old Persian rug now muffled her footsteps. She sank down in the chair placed underneath a black and white photo of men inside the interior of the bank circa 1910.

"Hello, folks." A tall, redheaded woman approached the other side of the wood banister, the start of a huge grin stretched across her perfect features. "I can't believe my eyes. Is that really you, Cole? Christine told me you were back in town. I wouldn't believe it if I weren't seeing it with my own eyes. And you must be Abby Bancroft. I'm Stacy Moore. Sorry about your grand-parents. That was so sad."

"Pleased to meet you and thanks." Abby stood and shook her extended hand. If she had to describe her in one word, it would be stunning. Not buying into the drab gray or blue that Abby associated with bankers, the woman's green suit accented her curves and brought out the golden highlights in her red hair. Pearls hugged her neck and ears and makeup covered any imperfections or freckles the woman might have. A feeling she recognized as jealousy, slapped her across her shoulders.

Abby deemed her skirt inadequate next to the tailored suit and expensive smelling perfume. Insecurity overshadowed her determination as childhood taunts and jeers crowded into her head. She hadn't been good enough then, would she be now? Normally, the five-inch difference wouldn't have bothered her, yet in this instance, Stacy's height complemented Cole's much better than her own. So did the idea that they had some sort of history together.

"Hi, Stacy. Long time no see."

Like Cole seemed to be doing, Abby held her breath, waiting for acceptance or rejection from Stacy. For Cole's sake, she hoped it was the former. His stance eased when the woman leaned over and gave him a hug. If it was hard for Abby to come to town as a complete stranger, it had to be doubly hard to come back where you grew up, but now had a bad reputation to live down. If she ever had a chance to meet Cole's ex-partner, she'd give him a piece of her mind.

"What am I thinking? Come in, please. What may I help you with today?" Stacy released Cole and opened the gate separating them. Abby had no doubts now why Cole had chosen this bank, even though Dynamite Creek boasted a population of 19,526. She hoped his instincts had been right. If they turned her down, Abby would have a hard time getting the house restored on what she had saved up.

"I'd like to open a checking account." Abby walked in ahead of Cole and waited for Stacy to close the half door behind them. Whatever her thoughts about the woman, she had to focus on the important stuff, like getting the loan. Neither her attire nor her past or her sudden insecurities mattered. She had to put everything aside and concentrate on her present need. "And apply for a home equity loan so I can restore the house and reopen the bed-and-

124

breakfast."

"A loan? I can see why. The Bancroft Mansion sure needs a lot of work. It's too bad that company —" Stacy's expression froze and horror leaped into her eyes. She placed a manicured hand on Cole's arm. "I'm so sorry, Cole. I wasn't thinking."

"It's okay, Stacy. I'm well aware of my reputation around here. I hope to change that by completing the contract." Cole shrugged out of her grasp. His words belied the turmoil Abby sensed from within him. She'd only known him a few days, yet an emotional string connected them that Abby suspected had nothing to do with the house.

"That's great. So that means you'll be around for a while, Cole. It'll be just like old times." Stacy recovered quickly and ushered them toward the rear of the area that didn't look too much different from the more public side.

Instead of teller stations, there were four large empty mahogany desks. The only signs of life were some personal effects that graced the scarred surfaces. A few potted trees were stationed to each side of the three large waist-high-to-ceiling windows framed with darkly stained slats of wood, and sunlight spilled through the top portions left uncovered by blinds and bathed everything in a golden glow. Even in this space, the antiquity hung heavy in the air.

"Where is everyone?" Abby asked. The place looked more like a mausoleum or museum instead of a bank. So far she'd only seen two people inside besides her and Cole, but if they would loan her the money she needed, Abby supposed it didn't matter.

"Matt's out sick and Lydia and Irene are at the middle school parent-teacher conferences. Daddy's here if I need some backup, but since most of the town seems to be doing something else today, I'm sure you'll be my only customers." Stacy stopped in front of a row of three oversized doors nestled amid more ornately carved wood molding.

Above the door, Vice President was painted in gold on the clear glass. Abby swallowed. "Nothing like going to the top," slipped from her lips.

"Stacy is the daughter of the bank president," Cole whispered in her ear as they passed through the open doorway and into a private office.

Leaving the door ajar, Stacy moved behind a grand mahogany desk and sat in the black leather chair. She motioned for them to sit across from her. "Don't pay attention to the words above the door. Daddy has a fascination with old things and wants to keep them as they are. I, on the other hand, wouldn't mind giving this place a major face-lift, bringing it into the twenty-first century."

"Why don't you tell us how you really feel? You were always good at that." Cole planted his elbows on his knees and rested his chin on his steepled fingers. From the corner of her eye, Abby saw the frown behind the fake grin plastered across Cole's lips.

"You know me too well, Cole Preston. Personally, I'd rather sell it and build a new branch on the vacant lot off Murphy Street. I don't know why you're wasting your time with the old stuff when you can start with a blank canvas." Stacy winked at him.

Abby's heart dropped to the rug beneath her feet and her fingers twisted around each other. Tension pierced the muscles between her shoulder blades and she fought to keep her jaw from flopping open. The idea that she didn't belong here exploded inside her brain. There had to be another bank and banker in the area that would share their vision for the Bancroft Mansion and not have their focus on Cole for more personal reasons.

"Because I believe in discovering and uncovering the beauty of what's already there instead of trying to create something artificial that has no substance or meaning. Now, if you don't mind, let's get down to business and take care of Abby's needs." Cole shifted back in his chair.

Abby didn't buy into his nonchalant posture or the silky, smooth tone of his voice that hinted at the anger simmering beneath the surface. Instinctively, she leaned toward him, glad he'd wanted to accompany her today.

"Look. I'll be honest with you. I can open a checking account, but the loan is probably going to be out of the question. Lending has tightened up and I presume you don't have a job if you intend to reopen the B and B. Without some sort of income, it's going to be difficult to approve you."

Abby's stomach dropped to the soles of her feet and her hands curled into fists. The eyes on the old painted portrait of a man behind Stacy's desk stared down at her as if mocking her attempts to establish herself in Dynamite Creek. Nonsense. Abby lifted her chin and straightened her shoulders. She refused to allow anything to come between her and her vision for the Bancroft Bed-and-Breakfast. "Then I'll take out a loan against my 401K and use the rest of my inheritance. I should have thought of that first. Sorry to bother you."

"Look, Abby, I want to help you but I have to do some research. Let me take your information and I'll see what I can do. It may take a few days though. In the meantime, you might want to check and see if you can get a small enterprise loan from the town."

Once outside the bank, Abby breathed in the crisp air. Now that she was the proud owner of a local checking account, some of the weight lifted from her shoulders. She'd made another step in cementing her presence here in town. Sunlight streamed across the blue sky and danced off the water in the small fountain on the snow-covered grass lawn of the public square. In a few days, she'd find out if she'd been approved for the loan. Despite the outcome, Abby would keep moving forward.

"There's not much else that can be done today that we can't put off until tomorrow." Cole said, guiding her down the steps and back onto the sidewalk. "Let me show you around a bit."

Abby nodded her approval. Having Cole at her side while she explored lessened her anxiety. Even after all the years of moving around, discovering new places should have been easy. Her nails dug into the fleshy part of her palm as the familiar sensation of a million butterflies trapped in her stomach took flight. Inhaling sharply, she fought for control. No one here would tease her or make fun of her. "Sounds great." Even though Abby hated shopping, and the thought of stepping in a store made her want to hyperventilate, she was curious about Cole. "You mentioned your sister has a shop around here. I'd love to see it."

"It's on the other side of the square. Hang on a second."

Cole fed two more coins into the meter as Abby looked toward the square and the large two-story structure in the center. Large trees lifted their bare branches to the sky, like multiple fingers reaching toward the sky. Aged pine trees added a spot of color to the surroundings as well as the green and red awnings protecting the windows of the businesses lining Main Street and the side streets surrounding the public building. A few minutes later, Abby and Cole stood beneath an oak tree.

"This is where they hold the Founder's Day Festival as well as other gatherings and various arts and craft shows." Cole's hand stiffened on her back.

With the festival only a few months away,

he should be back at the Bancroft Mansion stripping the floors or peeling away the tile on the dining room ceiling instead of wasting the rest of the afternoon trying to feel as if he fit in here. A sour taste filled his mouth. Despite the homey atmosphere, he never would belong in this tight-knit community that gave the illusion of welcome yet held the belief that if you slighted one, you slighted all.

He couldn't wait to leave, regardless of the fact that he then glanced over Abby's blond hair shimmering in the sun and breathed in her unique floral scent. He could neither deny his attraction to her nor the need to fix whatever problems haunted her.

"I can't wait." Her voice held excitement with an undercurrent of unease.

Cole could relate. He wrestled with his negative thoughts. Everything had happened for a reason. God had led him here to his hometown and would watch his back to make sure Cole accomplished what he set out to do. With God, anything was possible. And maybe part of the plan was for Cole to protect her and show Abby the power of His love. "It's going to be a challenge to get everything done, but we'll do it."

"I know we can do it." A smile lit her face

and Cole found himself glad to be on the receiving end. His day brightened.

"Come on, the shop is this way." He possessively placed his hand on the small of Abby's back again as if it permanently belonged there.

Wrong. It was only as temporary as the businesses lining the streets. As temporary as the smile on Mr. Milner's face for Abby, and the scowl reserved for Cole as the old man swept the sidewalk beneath the red-and-white barber pole in front of his shop. Cole had to step out of his way to avoid the well-worn bristles.

"That was rude. It kind of ruins the Norman Rockwell image." Abby stiffened.

"It does, doesn't it? But people here have long memories and hold even longer grudges." Cole continued to escort Abby down the sidewalk and away from the barber.

"Really?" Stopping in front of a knitting and loom shop, Abby whirled around to face him. "Well, that will change once you finish the house."

"Maybe it will." Cole wished he shared Abby's confidence. He wanted a piece of her optimism. Not that it mattered, because once he finished the B and B, aside from Abby and a few others, Dynamite Creek would be just another unpleasant memory to add to his already full album. "Come on, we're almost there."

The one-story structure with ornate carvings in the cement facing that housed his sister's shop still boasted the green and white striped awning. A little faded over time, but familiar, just as everything else. The buildings in town had remained the same, but had different businesses. One of the original hotels had become an antique mall, an old saloon had become an art gallery. His sister's shop had once been a beauty salon, but before that a drug store and before that a tailor's shop.

At the threshold of the Dynamite Creek Candle Company, Cole placed a hand on Abby's back, remembering her dislike of shopping. Suddenly, it was important to him to make her feel at ease. "Don't worry, not a clothing rack in sight in here but if you feel uncomfortable and need to leave, my sister will be okay with that."

"I think I'll be fine." Abby felt the heat creep to her cheeks. She appreciated Cole's concern, but hearing him voice it out loud made her feel foolish.

"I know you'll be fine, but I wanted to give you that option." He gave her a half grin. "If it makes you feel any better, I don't like spiders or scorpions, which unfortu-nately came with a contractor's territory."

"Fine. We'll make a good team then. You deal with the shopping and I'll deal with the creepy crawlies." The moment she said those words, Abby wanted to cram them back in her mouth. What she had suggested meant permanence. She backpedaled quickly. "For the time being, that is."

"Sounds like a plan." The amusement in his eyes dimmed. "Come on, let me show you Christine's shop."

A bell sounded when Cole opened the front door of the Dynamite Creek Candle Company and despite her earlier reserva-tions, Abby immediately fell in love with the interior of the shop when she stepped inside. Homey and welcoming, it was dif-ferent from any other store she'd ever visited. In fact, it didn't even feel like a store until she spied the cash register on the counter. Candles of various shapes and sizes and colors graced every tabletop and shelf. Raised panels on the side walls comple-mented the tin relief ceiling tiles and dark burgundy paint splashed the cement floor.

"Hello. I'll be right out." A voice floated from behind the back wall.

"No hurry, Christine, it's just us," Cole replied.

Abby picked up a pillar candle wrapped with a thin strip of wire with a heart charm delicately hanging down the side. She sniffed. Vanilla. Her favorite scent. She could envision it sitting on the mantle of her newly refinished fireplace in the parlor nestled in a multicolored glass bottom. With Cole at her side, the shop wasn't a nightmare darkening her day. And like he'd said earlier, not a clothing rack in sight. If he accompanied her on all her expeditions, she could probably get through it.

Abby took in the familiar scent of cinnamon as she picked up a three-wick candle with cinnamon sticks embedded in the sides. More candles of various shapes and sizes were strategically placed on the shelves of an antique cabinet, the beveled glass doors left open, inviting Abby to touch them.

Rustic iron crosses flanked the gold walls on each side and a round table with a glass top hosted candles with chili peppers decorating the tops and sides. Everywhere she looked, more candles and holders filled every available table and wall space.

"It's about time you came to see me." A woman hustled from the back and flung herself at Cole.

Abby's eyes widened and she had no

135

doubt they were siblings from their brunette hair to their light brown eyes. The striking similarities in their features and height astounded her.

"You must be Abby, I'm Christine." The woman released her brother and offered her a hand. Cole's sister wore a brightly colored peasant skirt, which complemented her frilly blouse. Dangling silver hoops hung from her pierced ears and bright pink lipstick coated her lips. "Cole didn't tell you that we were twins, did he?"

"No, he only mentioned you were his younger sister."

Christine batted his arm as the sound of Beethoven's Fifth Symphony from Cole's cell phone filled the air. "Only by five minutes."

"Five minutes or five years doesn't matter, I'm still the oldest." He tweaked his sister's nose in affection. "Excuse me a second, ladies."

As Cole grabbed his phone and glanced at the number, Abby noticed a look of surprise and disgust twist his features. His powerful strides ate up the distance to the front door. The bell chimed as he roughly pushed open the door. All Abby's shopping confidence exited with the man standing on the other side of the glass; his stance rigid, his shoulders tense.

"If you don't mind, I need to keep working. I have to take my daughter to the doctor today. You can come back to my studio and watch if you'd like." Christine motioned her to follow her.

"She's not sick, is she?"

"Oh, no. Thanks for your concern. It's time for her annual checkup." Christine's voice held a trace of laughter, similar to Cole's earlier. What else did the siblings have in common, and did Abby really want to find out?

She trailed the other woman, trying to take everything in. The front of the store contained the merchandise, but the back part sectioned off by a wall painted in faux gray, gold and silver housed the workshop where Christine made her creations. Bright lights contrasted with the cozy atmosphere out front and soft music filled the air. Candles in various stages of completion graced the worktables, and the utility shelves to her right were filled with more candles. A large refrigerator covered with her daughter's artwork dominated the back wall, right next to a four-burner stove.

"Your work is beautiful, and I see your daughter shares your talent." Abby sat down at the worktable. A tall candle sat in the center, surrounded by a few small jars of paint.

"Thanks. Nicole is a chip off the old block. Cole, too, in his own way. We all get our talent from our mother's side. I'm glad you're giving him a chance, Abby. Not many people in town will. Not after what happened." Christine tied an apron around her waist and sat down across from Abby. A sigh escaped her lips. "That's the unfortunate part of living here."

"I'm beginning to see that. It's like living in a fish bowl, isn't it?"

"Yes. I always managed to blend in, but even though we're twins, Cole's different. He had a hard time fitting in and making friends. I think our father and his defection had a lot to do with it. Things weren't the same once he was gone. My mom couldn't afford to buy us what the other kids had, and Cole took on odd jobs to help make ends meet. Kids back then were just as cruel as they are now. Even some of the adults made comments. They still do."

"I'm sorry to hear that." An unsettling feeling came over Abby at another thought that she and Cole had anything in common from their childhood. She didn't want to be any more aware of him than she already was because it would only make it harder when he left.

"While I've settled in, I think Cole is still trying to find his place in this world. I wish he'd give Dynamite Creek another chance, but I'd be happy if he found a permanent home somewhere instead of roaming around all the time. I've tried to get Cole to talk about it, but he won't talk to me. Maybe he will to you."

Abby's eyes widened and her jaw dropped open slightly. "I doubt that. We only talk about the house."

"Too bad. It's not healthy to hold everything inside." Christine reached over and patted Abby's arm. "If you ever need a listening ear, I'm your go-to gal. Now, enough about things we can't change." Christine picked up a fine-tipped paintbrush and dipped it into the silver paint. "Interesting, isn't it? Both Cole and I chose to work with our hands."

With precision strokes Christine applied the paint to the surface of the smooth wax.

"It is. You're both artists, but you work with different mediums." After a few moments of watching the other woman, Abby's curiosity got the better of her. "What are you making?"

"A wedding candle." Christine stuck the

139

tip of her tongue out as she worked, glancing briefly at the small white piece of paper that lay just off to the right with writing scribbled across the surface.

Cole had done the same thing when he'd been sitting at her kitchen table, outlining everything that needed to be done with her house. How alike they were in looks and personality quirks, and yet where Christine had chosen to stay in Dynamite Creek, Cole had taken on a nomadic life. What would it take for him to settle down? And did she really want him to?

Abby forced her mind back to their earlier discussion.

"A wedding candle? Really? I didn't realize they were handmade."

After another dip into the paint can, the other woman added more strokes of paint. She then turned the candle around so Abby could see the painting. A stylized silver cross took up two-thirds of the surface. "Some of them come from the stores, but I specialize in personalized ones. This is for my best friend's sister, Emma, who's getting married on Saturday."

"Wow. It's really beautiful." Abby tried to keep the wistfulness from her voice. If she ever got married, she'd ask Christine to make her a candle, too. Of course, that probably required a pastor and a church ceremony, which made her uncomfortable.

Christine's gaze softened as she dipped the paintbrush back in the jar and then delicately dabbed off the excess paint as she spoke. "If you want to see some of my work in use, I also made some of the candles inside my church. Maybe you can come to the service with us on Sunday. That would be a great way to meet more people in town and network a little. Unless of course, you've found another place to worship."

Abby squirmed, yet her curiosity won over. Maybe the more she learned. . . . "No, I haven't. I'll think about it."

Christine applied a few more delicate strokes. "I sense disquiet in you, Abby. You know Cole found God right before this whole thing with his ex-partner. It helped him through the rough spots. God can help you, too, if you let Him."

Compassion filled the other woman's brown eyes, reminding her of Cole. Christine set down the candle and paintbrush and placed her hand over Abby's. She squeezed gently, but instead of feeling comfort, Abby struggled for breath and the need to escape.

The bell over the front door chimed and in a few seconds, Cole stepped back into the room, a frown hugging his lips. "I'm back. Are you ready to go?"

Abby pulled her hand from beneath Christine's. This whole discussion had turned into something she wasn't quite ready to face yet. The need to change the conversation consumed her before the tidal wave of religion swept her into unknown depths that could drown her. "Yes. So who was on the phone?"

"My ex-partner, Robert."

CHAPTER SIX

"Robert?" Abby and Christine parroted as they stared at Cole.

The news erased the color from Christine's face while Abby's mouth dropped open. "What did he want?"

Cole paced from one end of the small workshop to the other in a few short steps. He wished for a bigger area but no amount of space would accommodate the thoughts whizzing by in his brain. Why did Robert contact him now? Why did he want to come back? More importantly, what was in it for Robert? Wedging his hand through his hair, Cole managed to keep his tone unemotional like he should do with his thoughts. "He wants to come and help."

Abby's mouth snapped shut.

"He wants to come back?" His sister wrapped her arms around her middle and shook her head vehemently. "Not a good idea. Definitely not a good idea."

"Cole, look at what he's done to you." Abby's eyes shone with concern. "You're not considering letting him come back, are you?"

Christine moved around the table and stood next to Abby; a wild and almost frightened look painted his sister's eyes a muddy brown, her face a stark white. "I'll second that, Cole."

The tension inside him increased. Cole pinched the bridge of his nose, the pressure relieving the pain building up in his forehead. Trapped between his sister and Abby in the front, the wall to his back and his ex-partner's words echoing in his brain, Cole wanted to get out of the shop, get out of Dynamite Creek. He couldn't leave until he finished the Bancroft Mansion.

"No. I told him we didn't need him." Except Cole really did. He needed Robert's expertise with the plaster and another set of hands to speed things along, but hearing Robert's voice only confirmed that Cole didn't want to see him again. Ever. He'd forgiven Robert and confirmed it every time he prayed, but that didn't mean he trusted him.

"Good. We *don't* need him, Cole. We can do it ourselves. Let's go back and get started then." Wrapping her arms around Christine, Abby gave her a hug. "It was great to meet you."

Dressed in an old pair of jeans and a ratty white T-shirt, Abby tied back her hair into a ponytail and bounded down the staircase to join Cole in the living room. The soft sunlight filtered in through the windows. Last night they'd moved the furniture into the parlor and covered it with old sheets Abby had found in a linen closet on the second floor.

"What do we do first?" She retrieved the cup of coffee she'd left on the mantel when she went upstairs to change after her morning jog. While the liquid had cooled slightly, the caffeine still did its work as she took another sip. The cobwebs cleared quickly, or maybe it was the man standing next to her that sharpened her focus.

Cole tied a bandanna around the top of his head and gave her one of his grins. Her heartbeat accelerated, which had nothing to do with the caffeine she'd consumed.

"Are you sure you're up to this?"

"Absolutely."

"Here, put this on then. It'll keep you from inhaling the dust and paint fumes." Cole handed her a white paper face mask before donning his own. His warm, brown

145

eyes watched her place the mask over her nose and mouth. He reached out and adjusted the elastic band before his fingers slid along her cheek and removed a loose tendril of hair and placed it behind her ear. Then they trailed slowly down the curve of her jaw and along her neck to finally rest on her shoulders. A raw whisper emerged from behind his mask. "I promise you everything will be okay, Abby. We'll get this house done on time."

Abby swallowed and nodded, not certain if she saw the hesitation in Cole's expression or if it was merely a play on the light filtering into the room. The weight of Cole's hands comforted her and when he squeezed gently, she thought he might pull her to him and kiss her, until she realized they both wore their masks.

His actions had nothing to do with any attraction on his end and only wishful thinking on hers. After her last boyfriend, she should know better. Heat flared in her cheeks, and she was glad Cole didn't have the ability to read her mind. "So, you never told me what we're going to do first?"

"We're going to remove the old paint from all the woodwork. It's messy, so I want to get it done before we rip up the carpet."

"That makes sense. It'll protect the wood floors."

His eyes twinkled. "I'll make you into a contractor yet. This way."

He led her to the tall window overlooking the street and handed her a pair of gloves and a scraper. He picked up a yellow rectangular tool by its handle and plugged the cord into a socket. "I'm going to heat the paint, and you're going to go behind me and scrape it off."

"Sounds tedious."

"It is, but this beats using chemicals and will make the good old-fashioned sanding easier." Cole readjusted the mask on his face. "Ready?"

Nodding, Abby donned the gloves. Tedious wasn't the only adjective Abby came up with thirty minutes later. Boring, mind-numbing and monotonous came pretty close behind. And as slow as the snails she'd watched as a kid in her mom's rented Beverly Hills yard.

Not the same zip code as that popular show years ago, but the attitudes of the kids blurred a lot of the boundaries. Her hands grew damp inside the work gloves. There were the haves and the have-nots and those in between. Those who blended in like a shadow in hopes no one would see them.

Abby fell into the second category and even though the years had dimmed the memories, they hovered near the surface and at times like this, exploded into jagged fragments of taunts, jeers and downright rudeness.

She forced away those thoughts like she did the bubbling paint. After she dumped the soft mass into the bucket, her gaze caught two grade school girls dressed in winter jackets walking down the sidewalk. Her heart ached when she saw a younger boy struggling to keep up. Abby winced and realized that action made Dynamite Creek more normal. Like everywhere else, the picture perfect town had a darker side that wasn't shown in the postcards and brochures. She saw it in the postures of the kids, and she'd seen it with the barber and Cole yesterday, and Christine had told her about Cole's troubled youth.

Out of the corner of her eye, she took in Cole's profile. The eyebrow she could see, furrowed in concentration. The muscles in his forearms flexed as he held the machine. In his silhouette, Abby saw Christine and the striking similarities between them, which only brought out how alone she was.

The last of the Bancroft line in Dynamite Creek and probably Arizona.

A very familiar position. Abby dumped more discarded paint. The gooey mass stuck to her scraper and Abby had to tap a few times to get off the various layers of whites, a light yellow and even a lilac color. Whoever thought of painting everything inside the house should have been tarred and feathered. The exposed wood underneath was gorgeous, and with a bit of sanding and a new coat of stain, it would really set off the stained-glass windows.

Cole had been right about wanting to restore the house instead of adding another coat of paint. There was a lot more to the man beside her than his outward appearance, and she found herself wanting to know more. "So, Cole, what was it like growing up with a sister?"

"She was a pain in my side, always following me around, wanting to do the same thing I was doing." The laugh lines etched into the corner of his eyes deepened. "There were times when I wished I was an only child, though. What was that like?"

"Lonely." Abby's shoulders sagged. "I always wanted a brother or sister, but my mom would just give me a melancholy smile and change the subject. After a while, I quit asking."

"I'm sorry. That must have been rough."

Cole moved the machine to another section. "You had friends though, didn't you?"

"Not really. We moved around a lot. My mom was like a hummingbird, flitting around always looking for something better." Abby ran her gloved fingers across the painted surface. How many times had mom looked out this window? What had she felt? What were her thoughts? Abby wished she could ask her mom about her life in Dynamite Creek and why she'd left. Maybe she could also have gotten some guidance with Cole but Abby had learned young that dreams and wishes were pretty much useless. "The only time she stayed put was when the cancer took over and she didn't have the energy anymore."

After Cole turned off the machine off and set it on the stepladder, he swiped away the beads of moisture gathering on his forehead while removing his face mask as Abby did hers. Stillness settled around them as if the house held its breath, waiting for something to happen. "How old were you when she died?"

"Eighteen years, two months and five days."

"I'm sorry, Abby." He gathered her in his arms and held her close.

With only a moment's hesitation, Abby

wrapped her arms around his waist and buried her head against his muscular chest. Awareness raced through her as she heard the steady thump of his heartbeat. Closing her eyes, she inhaled his masculine scent and imagined the man who held her wasn't just another temporary thing in her life of transients. For the time he held her she could imagine a tomorrow after tomorrow, and a tomorrow after that. Soon enough she'd wake up and Cole would be out of her life just like every other person who'd come to mean something to her.

Tears gathered in her eyes, but for this one glorious moment, the two of them shared a dance to the music they created in their loneliness, until she sensed Cole withdrawing. Something she expected eventually. Her head still cradled against him, her fingers played with the soft cotton fabric before she released herself from his grasp. "It's okay. I've had a while now to deal with it."

Wiping a few spots of paint from her bare arm, she stared up at him with hooded eyes. "My turn to ask another question. I've read that twins sometimes have a special language or way to communicate with each other that no one else understands. Is that true?"

"Christine and I do share a special bond. I'm not sure you'd call it a special language or not, but we always seemed to know each other's thoughts. My mom worked all the time and my dad was never around. When he left for good, my sister and I fended for ourselves a lot but she was always there for me and always will be. She'll be there for you too, and so will I as long as I'm here."

"I know. Thanks."

Another hush fell across the room and only dust particles hovered in the soft sunlight streaming in through the window. Cole reached out and pushed the loose strand of hair off her face again, his fingers testing the curl. It was all Abby could do not to turn her face into his palm and draw in the strength he emitted.

Placing his forefinger under her chin, Cole tilted back her head so she had no choice but to stare into his eyes. Hope deepened their brown color and his expression stilled and grew serious. "So is God, Abby. Even after all this happened with Robert, and I was alone in Phoenix dealing with the fallout, God was there for me. When you decide to accept the Lord and Jesus into your life, you'll find you're never truly alone, either."

Abby flinched and pulled away from Cole.

She wasn't ready to commit to something she didn't believe in yet, even though her mind had started to open to the possibilities. "We're burning daylight. At this rate we'll never get this done."

Time sifted faster than sand in an hourglass. Friday repeated Thursday, only that day, they'd managed to strip the windows in the parlor. Four windows in two days. He'd done part of the fireplace mantel this morning, but they still had six more windows on the main floor, thirteen on the second floor as well as all the doorways, the staircase and crown moldings. Cole's arms ached as he put down the finishing sander and pulled the mask from his face. The muscles in his back protested as he stretched his arms over his head. He hoped the rest of the house went quicker or Abby's guests would be helping with the renovation process.

Right now he had to go teach the kids' class at Lenny's hardware store. His gut clenched, knowing he should stay here, but the discount in supplies was well worth the four hours he spent away from his primary obligation. He headed toward the kitchen to wash his hands and tell Abby goodbye.

The only living thing in the back room was the small, furry white paw reaching across the table and swiping a piece of cereal out of Abby's china bowl.

"What?" Cole jumped. On Abby's seat, he could make out two ears flattened against the dark head of a cat and the beginnings of a hiss replaced the silence. "Get down."

The cat listened as well as most cats did, which was why Cole preferred dogs.

Large, green eyes now stared back at him and its scarred black nose quivered. His paw reached out and grabbed another square and pulled it to his mouth filled with sharp teeth. At this rate, there'd be nothing left for Abby.

The back door opened and in breezed Abby with a broom in her hand. "I see you met Cat. I finally convinced him to come inside. For a while anyway."

"Cat?" Cole waved his hand around Abby's food to keep the mangy cat from helping himself to more.

"Yes, silly name for him, don't you think? I'm going to call him Mittens because of his white paws. It's almost like he stepped in a can of paint somewhere because the rest of him is black." Abby replaced the broom in the closet and strolled into the room.

"How about if you don't call him anything at all and put him back outside where he belongs." The cat jumped on the table, sat down on his haunches and curled his front paws under his chest. His tail switched back and forth as his unblinking gaze creeped Cole out.

The crestfallen look on Abby's face put him back in his place. She picked up Mittens and cradled him to her chest, her chin rubbing the furry cat's head. Her fingers scratched him under his chin, causing an eruption of noise in the cat's throat.

Clarity struck him full force across his shoulders. The cat represented more than a creature with four legs. For Abby it meant permanence. "Sorry. It's your house, you can decide who gets to stay. Please eat before your cat decides to continue his meal. I just came in to tell you I'm leaving to do the workshop and will be back shortly after noon."

"I'm back." Cole stuck his head through the open office door, surprised to see Abby sitting at her desk, looking refreshed and almost downright perky. Even though Cole had gone next door to his temporary apartment and splashed water on his face, exhaustion clung to him, seeping from every pore. This house would be the death of him. So would his job at Lenny's.

"Good. I'll be ready to work in a moment." She gave him a smile that on a normal day would cause his blood pressure to rise. At this particular moment, it heated his blood, allowing Abby to scrape away the layers of old emotions and expose the raw, sensitive ones he'd buried years ago. Sort of like they were doing with the house, but unlike the wood, Cole wanted his assets to remain hidden.

"No hurry. What are you doing?" He moved in behind Abby and fought the urge to place his hands on her shoulders. They weren't a couple, just two people working together toward a common goal. At the end of the project, he'd be gone.

"I'm building a website. It's amazing what I can do with a simple and free program. I can't believe my grandparents never had one." Abby clicked the cursor over the save button and rolled back in her chair, barely missing his foot. She glanced up at Cole.

"I don't think Charles and Sally cared too much for technology." He pointed to the rotary telephone to make his point. "They probably survived by word of mouth and recommendations."

Cole moved away from Abby's warmth and sat on the edge of the desk, needing the clarity of distance. Taking reservations and creating a website cemented the Founder's Day Festival grand reopening for the B and B. He shoved a hand through his hair determined to make the deadline despite his commitment to Lenny. Sleep was a waste of time anyway. "Can I ask you a question?"

"Sure."

"How are you going to manage photos when everything is so — so — outdated?"

"I'm only doing the prep work and I'm using the old photo from the original brochure. I'll drop in the rest of the pictures when we finish. The important thing is to get a presence on the web to draw in extra business. How was your first day at Lenny's?"

More tension whacked Cole between his shoulder blades. The air around him had been charged with negative whispers and stares of the parents. Toward the end, the scale tilted toward being more positive but it would take a lot more to regain everyone's trust. "Great. I had fifteen kids show up." But that wasn't what bothered him.

"That's wonderful. Next time I bet you'll have thirty." Her smile only increased his stress. "Okay, I'm ready to work. Why don't you go change and we'll get started."

"Abby, I have to go back and cover for

Lenny this afternoon. He has a funeral to go to."

His haggard voice dripped with a harshness he couldn't contain. He should have called with the news instead of telling her in person, but he wasn't that type. Cole should have known that when he agreed to do the workshops that it wouldn't stop there. Little by little, a funeral here, a doctor's appointment there, he'd be working at the shop instead of fulfilling his commitment to Abby. The weight of the house, Robert's phone call and everything else going on came crashing down on him.

His attraction to Abby didn't help matters, either.

Abby stood, the squeak of the chair muffled against the carpet, yet loud enough to compete with their ragged breathing. She stepped forward and reached out to place her hands on his shoulders, her disappointed gaze never leaving his. Cole's muscles bunched beneath her fingers, yet he was unable to pull away. "Of course you have to go. The house can wait."

"You're okay with that?" He focused on her lips and the way they tilted up, her scent, a hint of fresh berries and fragrant soap, and her hair, only a clip away from bouncing around her slight shoulders. He

wanted to run his fingers through its softness and slant his lips over hers and taste
her, touch her, brand her and make her his.
Forget he wasn't marriage material or that
temporary was only a state of being.

"I'd be lying if I said yes, but you made
the commitment to Lenny as you have to
me. I wouldn't expect you to back out on
either one of us."

"You're something else." Encircling her
elbows he teased her forward and leaned
close with barely a millimeter between
them. Her eyelids fluttered down, and her
lips parted, inviting him to partake in her
offering. A soft moan escaped her lips,
expelled on a breath of helpless need that
matched his own.

His cell phone rang and stopped him from
making a huge mistake. Abby's expression
crumbled when Cole stepped back, breaking the connection. What was he thinking?
Kissing Abby Bancroft should be the last
thing on his mind. He wasn't marriage
material and he shouldn't be leading his
temporary boss down a path he couldn't
remain on for the long haul. His gaze swept
Abby's and he saw her vulnerability before
she masked it with a cool level of efficiency.

Too bad he couldn't do the same.

He glanced at the number and pushed the

ignore button. Why was Robert calling him again?

A knock on the front door surprised Abby as she worked at her computer putting in more information on her website. Irritated at the interruption, she shoved her chair back. She wasn't expecting anyone and Cole had his own key now, but he wouldn't be back for at least another hour. Another Kitty Carlton? Or a door-to-door salesman, if they even existed anymore.

The bolt slid back easily now that Cole had changed out the locks, and the door swung open on newly oiled hinges. A man a few years older than Cole stood on the porch, his fingers clutched around a small brown paper bag until his knuckles gleamed white. Shadows clung to the delicate skin under his eyes, and touches of gray lightened his blond hair. Fatigue lines bracketed his lips and hesitation lodged in his green eyes. Nervousness implanted itself in Abby's stomach and she wished Cole stood by her side.

"May I help you?"

"Yes, I'm looking for Cole Preston." The man's gaze spun around the reception hall, his eyes widening slightly.

"He's working in back right now. Is there

something I can do for you?" Abby gripped the door tighter and started to shut it in his face, her unease rising. The stranger wore a look of desperation, and suddenly the town didn't feel as safe as when she'd drove in last week.

"My business is with Cole." The man shuffled his fingers through his unkempt hair and shifted on his feet. "Can I talk to him?"

"No. He's busy." There was no way Abby was going to let the man know Cole wasn't inside the house with her. "Come back after five and he'll be available."

"How about the Bancrofts then? I need to talk to someone."

Abby took a territorial stance, her unease pushed aside by her rising irritation. The man disturbed her afternoon and didn't know how to take a hint to go away. Her fingers clenched harder around the door-knob, ready to shove the door closed despite how it might impact her reputation. "They're dead. This is my home now. Just who are you?"

The stranger's composure crumbled. "Robert Meade. Cole's ex-partner."

Temporary anger curled around her heart at the man's audacity. First the phone calls and now this, yet he'd come back for a reason. Why? "But —"

"I know he doesn't want to see me but I need to see him. I came back to help him. I need to explain." Robert looked at the bag in his hand before he thrust it at her. "Here, if you're the new owner, this is for you. It's not much, but it's a start. I'm sorry."

Her hand trembled visibly as she reached out and grabbed it. When Abby looked inside, her anger and uneasiness morphed into shock and she felt the blood drain from her cheeks. She reached inside and pulled out two bundles of strapped one hundred dollar bills. Four thousand dollars if she could believe the dollar amount stamped on the wrapper. She wavered on unsteady feet as if the muscles in her legs refused to work.

Alarm elevated her blood pressure. Abby dropped the bag and thrust the bundles back at him. Her words choked her. "Where did you get this?"

Robert stared at the bills in his hand before his anguished look returned to her. "I — things —" He held out the money again. "Please. Take it. Look. Like I told Cole, I've changed. I had a 'come to Jesus meeting' a few months back. As for this, I earned it working a remodel job in Phoenix. As soon as it was finished, I came up here to take care of some unfinished business."

He looked around the reception hall again. "Cole needs my help. Without a crew, he'll never get this place done."

Abby stared at the money and hated knowing that she needed it. The bank had called yesterday and denied her application. The only choice she had now was to contact the city or find a private loan. Taking Robert's money would be a short-term solution. Indecision tore at her insides. She had no way to verify Robert's words unless she called whatever number he gave her, which could easily be a setup as well. The four thousand dollars would certainly help with the materials and the extra help with the house so she had a chance of reopening on schedule. She had reservations to honor and guests to take care of. Plus the fact that Cole would work himself to death to take care of her impossible, yet necessary, timeline. She couldn't have that on her conscience.

Cole would be angry if she let Robert in the house but the money and Robert's knowledge would go a long way in helping out. Abby caught a glimpse of Robert's hands. Tiny scars bisected each other and a fresh scrape had crusted over on his left knuckle. A roughness that could only come from working chafed his skin. He stared at her, his expression still bordering on desperation. Her blood continued to rush through her veins at a dizzying speed.

Making her decision, she grabbed the bundles with trembling fingers and tucked them in her pocket. "I'm still not one hundred percent sure about this but Cole needs the help. I'm doing this for him, not you and I'm only taking the money because it rightfully belongs to me."

His gaze swept the floor. "I'm sorry, Ms. Bancroft. I've got a lot of explaining to do."

"You do, but not to me." Concern curled around her heart. Thoughts of how some of the people in Dynamite Creek treated Cole when it should be Robert on the receiving end pummeled her emotions. Abby flipped her ponytail behind her shoulder and lifted her chin. "You need to make it right with Cole."

"I know. And he's not the only one." Self-disgust crossed his features and his voice cracked. "Please believe me when I tell you I've changed."

"Then I guess you'd better get your work clothes on and get started. Cole left off in the parlor."

A brief silence filled the area around them. She'd been down the sincerity road before with her mother. All promises of permanence broken on a whim or when something better came long. Abby drew in a ragged breath and hoped she didn't live to regret her decision to make Cole's life a bit easier.

CHAPTER SEVEN

"You're back?" Abby's eyes widened when Cole stepped into the mudroom. She glanced at her watch after she set down the pitcher of iced tea next to two glasses on the serving tray on the counter. "I — I wasn't expecting you for a while."

Fatigued, Cole closed the back door behind him and moved into the kitchen. With a normal eight-hour day already behind him, Cole still had another four or five hours of paint stripping ahead. Blood disappeared from Abby's cheeks as she wiped her hands across her jeans. Her actions sent up a red flag that things weren't quite the same way he'd left them a few hours ago, especially when he spied the tray on the counter with two glasses of iced tea on it. "I am. Lenny got back in time to close up. You have company?"

Footsteps on the hardwood floor from what sounded like the dining room confirmed his question. Abby worried her bottom lip, tucked her fists into her pockets and rocked back on her heels. "I do —"

From her reaction Cole guessed it was another man. He should be happy Abby decided to date, but a spurt of jealousy filled him. "Then I guess I should go."

"Cole, wait." She stopped him with her hand before he could retreat outside. "I — it's Robert."

This time it was Cole's turn to falter. "You let him in here?"

"What was I supposed to do? He showed up out of the blue. With some money I might add."

Cole thrust a hand through his hair and looked past the compassion written in Abby's eyes. Bile choked his throat, making it difficult to breathe. "You could have turned him away."

"I tried, but he's as persistent as someone else I know." Abby stepped in front of him, blocking his path into the hall. "He's here, Cole, and I want him to help. I did it for you. There's no way you can get this place done by yourself. And like you said, we need his expertise on the plastering, and another pair of hands will only help us."

Footsteps echoed on the hardwood floor behind them and stopped at the threshold of the room. "Is there a problem, Abby?"

"Robert." Cole almost didn't recognize his ex-partner. His heart pounded. After all these months, he didn't know what to expect, or how he'd feel seeing the person who'd dragged his name through the mud and emptied out his bank account. Sweat beaded on his forehead. He'd forgiven Robert, yet facing him still upset the delicate balance he'd struggled to maintain.

A cautious smile echoed Robert's stance and the waiver in his voice. "In person. Hi, Cole. It's good to see you again."

Cole shifted, causing the floorboards beneath him to squeak. He'd prayed for some help with the house multiple times daily and apparently, this was God's answer. His hands clenched and unclenched, still uncertain. Months of agony, uncertainty and doubt dogged him, and Cole's emotions tumbled together, mixing and blending like paint in a can until two emotions remained.

Forgiveness and distrust.

"I guess we'll be working together again for the time being." His gaze swept over Abby and his heart ached. He wanted to believe that she had done this for his own benefit, yet his trust in her was gone, too.

■ ■ ■ ■

Abby retreated to the back porch to give Cole and Robert some time to talk. Indecision still clawed at her insides. Had she made the right choice by allowing Robert inside? Did she really need the money that badly or Cole the help when she worked alongside him? Cole's initial reaction had been shock, she couldn't blame him there, but his lukewarm reception of his ex-partner and then the way his expression filled with distrust when he stared at her, left her saddened and tired. She was only trying to help.

"Yoo-hoo, dearie, over here." Mrs. Wendt waved from her back porch. "How are you doing this afternoon? How's the house coming along?"

Abby sat on the steps and waved back. She tried to raise a smile, but fell short. "Hi, Mrs. Wendt. Just fine and the house looks great. How about yourself?"

"Just fine, dearie. The Lord has given us another beautiful day and what looks to be another beautiful sunset. Hang on a second, I have something for you."

A high-pitched series of barks combined with a low growl erupted from Mrs. Froehlich's yard. Movement from the right side

169

caught Abby's peripheral view. His tail puffed up and his ears flattened against his skull, Mittens came tearing through the hedge and skittered up the steps to cower behind Abby. Laughter bubbled from her lips as she grabbed the cat and pulled him onto her lap. Her fingers stroked the fur, trying to pat it back into place. "Why, Mittens, I can't believe you're afraid of that fluffy little dog."

"Fifi, come back here." Mrs. Froehlich wedged herself between the tiny opening in the hedge.

Glad to have something else to occupy her mind, Abby stood and watched both her neighbors march from opposite directions toward her, each of them carrying a plate of food. Abby would have to go on a diet if this continued.

"Ankle biter, that's what Fifi is." Mrs. Wendt hefted herself up the steps. "Who in this day and age names their poodle Fifi? It's so cliché."

"I'll give you cliché, Helen." Mrs. Froehlich huffed, scooped up her dog in one hand and followed Abby's other neighbor across the porch to stand on her other side. "And he's not an ankle biter. Those are love nips."

"Ankle biter." Mrs. Wendt seethed. "I've

got scars to prove it."

"Love nips. Maybe if you'd stop cutting through my backyard every week, Fifi might leave you alone." Mrs. Froehlich set her plate on the railing before she stroked her dog's fur.

Sure of the cat's safety, Abby put him down and stood between the two women, breaking the tension slightly. Her head spun wildly with this new experience and it was all Abby could do to not to place her hands over her ears and block out the bickering. "Mrs. Wendt, Mrs. Froehlich, please stop arguing. If it makes any difference, I'm calling the cat Mittens. Now that's a cliché if I ever heard one."

"Oh, dear. She's right." Mrs. Wendt giggled as a smile split her lips. "I thought we agreed you'd call me Helen, though. It's more neighborly, don't you think, Betty?"

"Absolutely, and you're to call me Betty, remember?"

Abby's gaze trailed after Mittens as he disappeared beneath the hedge again. She longed to do the same just as she'd done in the past. As her mother had done before her. A realization crystallized in her brain. Now she understood part of her mother's behavior. When faced with confrontation or any type of unease, Sharon hightailed it to the next town. Abby didn't have that luxury anymore. Determined to stay in one place now, she needed to placate her new neighbors and redirect their attention. "Sorry, Helen. Sorry, Betty. What have you brought for me today?"

"Banana bread." Both women preened at the same time.

"My world famous banana bread. Won the blue ribbon at the Founder's Day Festival last year." Betty picked up her plate and thrust it into Abby's hands.

"Only because she was married to one of the judges." Helen sniffed and settled her plate on top of Betty's.

Abby's stomach did another nosedive. "I'm sure they're both wonderful. If it's anything like your tuna casserole, I can see why it won a prize. And Helen, Cole and I ate yours the day you brought it over. Now if you both don't mind, I've got a lot of work to do on the house."

"Oh, dear. Don't mind us old biddies then, putting ourselves in the forefront instead of thinking of you. Now, if you need any help cleaning up or redoing the shelf liners in the cupboards, just let us know. We've got a lot of time on our hands since Jessica and Troy moved to the Valley."

"Jessica and Troy?"

"Our grandchildren. My sweet Jessica ran off with her Troy right out of college." Helen pointed at Betty. "I still think she settled."

"If anyone settled, it was my Troy." Betty folded her arms across her ample chest and stared darkly at Helen.

"Wait a minute. You're related?" Abby broke in, her mind still whirling with the implications. Suddenly, both plates weighed down her arms as if filled with the animosity between her two neighbors.

"In-laws or outlaws as the case may be. Best friends until that happened," Betty replied. "She's just miffed because she can't meddle in their lives anymore. I say she scared them away."

Her gaze ping-ponged back to Helen, and she retreated a step backward in hopes of being able to slip into the house undetected.

"I did not scare them away. The reason they moved is because there's a lot more job opportunities in Phoenix, but that's neither here nor there. So, is there a man in your life, Abby?"

Abby didn't like the new direction the conversation had taken, either. Her private life was private and shouldn't be up for discussion. "No. There's no man."

Speculation returned to the woman's eyes. "Wonderful. This town is perfect for finding your heart's desire and it helps to have one right under your nose."

"Cole's not my type and I'm not looking for any relationship right now. Neither is he," Abby protested.

"Right. Every single girl is looking for someone special. Sometimes they just need a little help. Are you in or out, Ms. Fifi two-shoes?" Helen asked, ignoring Abby's statement.

"I'm in, of course." Betty stepped past Abby to stand next to Helen. Their heads dipped together, making the turbulence in Abby's stomach grow. She didn't like the conspiratorial glances in her direction.

"No, no, no. A way to a man's heart is through his stomach. It certainly worked with Phillip." A smug grin hugged Helen's lips. "Of course he wasn't always so um — un-thin."

"Don't I know it. I suppose you do have a point." Betty nodded.

The two women appeared to be getting along now which should have warmed Abby, yet she didn't like or appreciate how they talked about her as if she weren't there. Her fingers tightened around the plates. Abby had heard those words about food and men before, but in her practical mind and thanks to her knowledge of basic anatomy, she knew the heart and stomach were not really connected. Helen's words continued to ring in Abby's ears, though. From her one experience at their house when she went to borrow a cup of milk, she knew Helen and Phillip complemented each other. Finished each other's sentences. Knew each other so well, they almost started to resemble their other half.

All of a sudden, Abby wanted that for herself. One day. After she settled in. After she reopened her business. After she learned how to fully trust again. But that special person wasn't Cole even though his presence did funny things to her insides.

In a way, maybe it was true that a way to a man's heart was through his stomach. It wasn't a physical connection but an emotional one. Abby had felt the love with each bite of banana bread Betty had baked and each mouthful of tuna casserole Helen had prepared. Not that she hadn't felt loved by her mother, but her two neighbors's contributions were different in a way she couldn't describe.

Like her mom, Abby didn't possess a cooking gene though Abby knew that wasn't the reason why Sharon had never found a husband. She'd just picked wrong. The men her mom dragged through Abby's life never stayed long enough to wear out their welcome and Cole wasn't the permanent hang-your-hat-up-and-stay-a-while kind of guy, either.

Abby didn't want to face the same lonely existence her mother did and die alone while her daughter was at work. Her eyes welled and she fought to keep the tears from sliding down her cheek. She would make different choices.

"But I think in this case, it's going to take more."

In what case? Abby forced her attention back to the conversation instead of dwelling on the past. The women discussed her as if she were a commodity, not a human with thoughts and feelings. She walked over to the small patio table and set down the plates, not sure she could hold them anymore and not wanting to drop the food they held.

"Like what?"

Yeah. Like what?

"Well, look at her. High cheekbones, gorgeous eyes and a figure that's hidden beneath T-shirts and coveralls. A little makeup and the right clothes would do wonders." Betty mimicked an hourglass with her hands.

"Well, what do you expect? She's remodeling the house. I wouldn't put on my Sunday best for that. I still say it's through the stomach."

"Looks."

"Stomach, I tell you."

"Looks. Abby definitely has those. If she'd use them to her advantage, she could snag a man."

"Stop it, ladies. You're both wrong." Cole materialized in the kitchen doorway, his arms crossed in front of his muscular chest. "The way to a man's heart isn't food or looks, or anything so superficial."

Both women turned to face Cole. "Then what is it?" Helen wore a smirk.

Cole tsked, his lips twisting into Abby's favorite grin. Her heart fluttered again and her breathing became impossible.

"After nearly forty years of marriage, I would have thought you'd have figured it out." He stepped across the porch, moved in beside Abby and hesitated a moment before he placed his arm around her waist. His warm breath fanned her hair. "It's the little things like a touch or a glance. Sharing an opinion. Lending a helping hand. Worrying about them when they go for a jog."

Abby filled the silence by adding her thoughts. "Holding open the car door or helping someone across the street. Listening and just being there and finding help in unexpected places." She stared at Cole's deepening dimples and ever-present five-o'clock shadow. She inhaled his masculine scent, which sent another bolt of awareness through her veins.

"Respect and forgiveness." His gaze captured hers and Abby found herself falling into the apology written in the earthy depths of his eyes. The world around them ceased, the two bickering women falling away as he reached up and tenderly pushed a strand of hair behind her ear. His voice husky with emotion, he continued, "Like using china instead of paper."

A slight breeze stirred the tree branches to their right, breaking the spell. Abby shook her head to clear the remnants of what just passed between them. "Now, if you'll excuse us, we've got a lot of work to do. Thanks for the banana bread. I doubt it will last the night."

"Really? We'll have to remember that, won't we, Betty?"

Arm in arm, Betty and Helen descended the steps together, their heads bent toward each other, still in a heavy discussion.

Abby broke from Cole's embrace and shook her head after the two women left. "Thanks for rescuing me."

"No problem. Except I think I've given those two busybodies something to chew on. I don't think we've seen the last of them."

"Unfortunately, I think you're right. They are my neighbors, you know. And one is your landlady." She scooped up the plates.

"Fortunately for me, it's only temporary. Look, I'm sorry I reacted so badly. Having Robert back was kind of a shocker. I'm not sure it's the best decision but I realize you're only thinking of me." Cole held open the screen door for her.

His words reinforced his short-term status and regret permeated through her that even the touch of his hand on her arm couldn't chase away.

Quietness slipped around Abby as she entered the house after her morning jog on Sunday. No sander, no scraping, no voices, just peace until she looked at the mess in the parlor and living room. She inhaled the scent of old paint and took in the areas of bare wood peeking through the peeled paint that remained. She didn't need the reminder of how much work still needed to be done, yet both Cole and Robert had taken a few hours off to go to the church service she'd gracefully declined to attend, despite Christine's invitation.

Her sneakers squeaked against the worn wood floor of the hallway as she headed toward the kitchen. Cole had told her that refinishing the floors would be the last thing done, which made sense because Abby knew painting could get messy. Each time she'd moved, she'd painted her new apartment, trying to create the permanence and sense of belonging she craved. No matter how careful she was, paint dusted her hair, her clothes and the floor. She suspected painting this place would be no different with the exception that it belonged to her.

Would Robert's help be enough to get the Bancroft Bed-and-Breakfast ready to open by the Founder's Day Festival? Abby had no clue, but she suspected they needed help. Help cost money. Wages she couldn't afford because she hadn't gotten the loan. Abby had Robert's cash though, which he'd told her to use to buy linens and other accessories. Would he be okay if she used it to pay for temporary labor? Her runner's euphoria disappeared like the bead of sweat she'd just wiped from her brow. Anxiety twisted her stomach into a pretzel and the four walls crowded in on her.

She couldn't afford not to open on time.

Grabbing a fresh cup of coffee, Abby

stepped onto the back porch and drew in the underlying scent of the dew-kissed morning as she sat down on the wooden step. Wedging her trembling elbows on her knees, she sipped the steaming brew and watched two rabbits scamper under the pine tree. Her shoulders hunched. At times like this she missed her mother and their long talks and crazy advice. Any advice would be better than none at all. Suddenly Abby had the ache to get in her car and take a long, scenic drive.

Cole had told her that with God, she'd never be alone. Was it really that simple? Mom had believed but she'd lost her battle with cancer, yet up until the day she'd died, she'd prayed for peace and an end to her suffering. Had God's answer been to take her home to Him?

If that were the case, then He'd taken the only family Abby had, and that was why she didn't believe. In anguish, she stared at the large tree dominating her backyard, its bare branches lifting to the sky, open and inviting prayer, full of hope and promise. She still didn't quite buy into the religion part, yet small things, like the thoughts that just passed through her brain, teased her into rediscovering more. The beauty of the mountains, so diverse from the ocean where she grew up, astounded her. All the plants and animals and other wondrous things didn't appear here by accident.

Confusion wreaked the peacefulness of her surroundings. Next week she would accept Christine's invitation to attend the church service.

The next Sunday came quicker than Abby had anticipated. With Robert's help, they'd managed to strip all the downstairs windows and door framing, despite the extra hours Cole had to put in at Lenny's. The wallpaper in both the reception area and parlor had been removed, revealing more plaster damage and a paint job that left a lot to be desired. Either her ancestors had been color-blind, or there had been a huge sale on lavender-colored paint.

Taking a day off to appease Cole and get away from the house was just what Abby needed right now, though she would rather spend it exploring her surroundings than going to church. Too bad Cole had driven today or she might have just pulled out of the parking lot and never looked back. Even shopping would be preferable. Real shopping, not the window-shopping from her youth where all she could do was stand on the outside and dream of buying the current fashions instead of rummaging through the used clothing rack at the local thrift store. She wondered where the nearest secondhand store was in Dynamite Creek. Old habits died hard. So did the idea of going inside the building fifty yards away.

"We're here." Cole undid his seat belt and touched her arm.

"So we are." Her fingers bit into her palm. The last time she'd stepped inside a church had been for her mother's funeral. Sadness only increased her apprehension. Coming to a strange town had been one huge uncomfortable event. Attending the church on the outskirts of town really put her beyond her comfort zone. Abby had made the commitment to come and she knew it would be good for her to meet more people. She also wanted to see Christine again.

"I'm here for you, Abby. So is Christine and everyone else around you." He helped her from his truck.

The church surprised her though with it newness compared to a lot of the buildings she'd seen near the downtown area. The one-story red brick building with its shingled roof was a far cry from the stucco Spanish-style building she'd passed every day in Santa Monica on her daily jog.

Cole's hand on the small of her back

comforted her as they made their way across the pavement and up the three cement stairs even though she suspected it was there more to keep her from bolting from the scene. The butterflies in her stomach increased and she leaned into his palm, glad for his presence and that she hadn't driven herself here. If she had, she'd probably still be in her red Escort, her white knuckles fused around the steering wheel.

Abby stopped before she entered through the open massive double doors. She couldn't do this. She felt the blood drain from her face and pool around her ankles.

"Everything okay?" Cole gently pulled her to the side and out of the stream of the other worshipers.

Her mouth opened, but the words stuck in her throat. Her gaze skittered to Cole's before she dropped it to stare at the beige "Welcome" mat next to her feet. He wouldn't understand her panic.

His fingers gently elevated her chin; his eyes brimmed with tenderness and understanding. "Look, Abby. I'm glad you made it this far. You don't have to attend if it's too uncomfortable for you. You can wait in the community room with some coffee and I'll come find you after the service. It would mean a lot to Christine if you came though."

A small sigh floated between them as he caressed the smooth skin beneath her chin. He dipped his head closer, until the warmth of his breath touched her cheek, causing the blood to rush back to her face. "If it makes you feel better, the Wendts and the Froehlichs will be here and so will my mom and stepfather. I'm sure we can all sit together if we get inside soon."

"Your mom still lives here?" Cole's admission surprised her. She searched his expression and only found regret. Had this whole incident with Robert damaged his relationship with his mother? What else had it done? Was there any way Abby could help mend the rift?

"Yes. Now if you're ready?"

Abby nodded, a strange emotion overcoming her, as her feet seemed to move independently of her brain and led her inside. An inexplicable feeling that she belonged here consumed her and chased away any lingering doubt. Instead of heading to the left where she spied rows of tables in the community room, she went straight, as if she'd been here many times before, the pull of the organ music impossible to ignore.

The attorney's assistant, Delia, stood with a man by the doors leading into the worship area. She handed her a bulletin along with a big smile. "Abby. It's great to see you again. We're so glad you could join us today."

"It's good to see you, too," Abby responded.

"This is my husband, Tyler. Tyler, Abby Bancroft."

"Pleased to meet you." They both spoke at the same time as Abby extended her hand to the dark-haired man. She liked him immediately and could see why the petite blonde had fallen for him.

"And this is Cole Preston. He's the contractor working on my house." Abby turned their attention to Cole, who stood quietly beside her.

"Welcome," Tyler spoke and reached into his shirt pocket to pull out a business card. "I know this isn't the time or place, but I'm a plumber. Just starting out on my own. If you need any help or want an inspection on the house, I'll give you a good price."

"Thanks." Cole tucked the card into his own pocket. "I'll give you a call. After you?"

Inside the church the people didn't judge Cole and seemed to accept him, which filled Abby with warmth. They accepted her too just as God seemed to be doing. Stepping on the light beige carpet, Abby was surprised when lightning didn't strike or the ceiling didn't collapse on her or Robert, who sat alone in the back corner. She gave him a tiny wave. Maybe God was as forgiving as she'd been told. Maybe He'd forgiven her? Maybe He was glad she'd walked inside even though uncertainty still existed.

Her gaze wandered back to the interior. Partially filled light wood pews flanked either side of the aisle and beautifully painted tall white candles that Abby recognized as Christine's work graced the two candleholders on each side of the pulpit. Three large narrow windows allowed sunlight to stream in, the soft shafts of light almost dancing on the stairs leading up to the altar. Off to her right, she saw a brightly dressed middle-aged woman behind the organ.

"Here." Cole ushered her into a pew seven rows from the front. The Wendts sat behind them, and the Froehlichs farther down in the same row. Abby smiled and wiggled her fingers at them despite the fact each woman's smug grin irked her.

"Abby," Christine called out from her position at the end of the pew. She stood and hugged her. "I'm so glad you could make it." She pointed to the people who sat with her. "This is my daughter, Nicole, our mother, Annette and stepfather, Manny Garza."

She introduced them to what looked to be a nine-year-old girl that resembled both Cole and Christine with her dark hair and dimples, yet her unusual violet eyes contrasted against the paleness of her skin and accented the freckles sprinkling her cheeks and nose. The balding Hispanic man in his early sixties greeted her with a friendly smile as he wrapped his arm protectively around his wife's waist. Abby's gaze froze on the striking brunette woman in the dark green pants suit. An older version of Christine stared back at her, yet the years had been kind. Only a few faint wrinkles lined her blue eyes and lightly tinted lips.

"Hi. Pleased to meet you."

"Hi." Annette's soft, shy, melodic voice responded back to her. Her expression wore the innocence of Nicole's. "You must be Christine's new friend. Is this your husband?"

Abby fought to contain her surprise and concern. "No. It's Cole, your —"

"The service is starting. I'll explain later." Cole sat down and pulled Abby with him.

Once the service was finished, Abby breathed a sigh of relief. Yet she felt a connection, something she couldn't quite put her finger on. The pastor's sermon on forgiveness struck a chord with her, and if she wasn't mistaken, everyone in the congregation. Would she be able to forgive everyone who had done her wrong? Like her mother for dying, her grandparents for not looking for her, all the children who made fun of her and Robert for stealing from her family? More important, would God really forgive her for not believing in Him and turning away?

She wondered if she wore the same dazed expression as Annette, her fingers entwined with Manny's, who sat on the other side of her.

Cole must have seen her questioning gaze because he dipped his head toward her, his voice filled with pain. "My mother was in a car accident several years ago. She suffered a severe head injury and now has the mental capacity of an eight-year-old. Some days she doesn't even recognize that she has a husband who adores her."

Abby's heart ached as she gazed at the anguish creasing his features. Her fingers longed to wipe away the sadness. "She doesn't remember you, does she?"

Cole shook his head. "No. I've been gone too long."

"I'm so sorry, Cole." Abby took his hand in hers and squeezed gently.

CHAPTER EIGHT

"May I talk to you a second?" Pastor Matt Henning stopped Cole in the entryway to the community room where most of the congregation had stopped for coffee and snacks. Only a decade or so older than Cole, the other man had a welcoming face and a smile to go with the receding hairline which had started to gray at the temples.

"Sure." Cole moved to the right, just outside the double doors, his gaze not straying too far from where Abby, his sister and niece stood in line for refreshments. Manny had already left with his mother because she felt one of her almost daily headaches coming on and Robert had slipped out right as the service had ended. He still wasn't sure how he felt about the whole Robert incident, and Abby's role in it. His trust in her wavered, but he knew how charismatic and persuasive his ex-partner could be. He thrust those thoughts aside because they didn't belong in His house.

"I'm glad you worshiped with us today. I know Christine is really happy you've come back, even if it is just temporarily."

"In a way it's good to be back." The idea took him by surprise. Peace settled across Cole's soul as another member of the congregation, Mr. Pratt, smiled and waved. No animosity this morning, which brightened his day, especially after the blank look his mother had given him. "What did you need to talk to me about? I've got to get back to work on Abby's house."

"Well, I don't think you know but I also run the youth ministry here. The kids and I have come up with a project which will include some of the at-risk youth in the surrounding communities." Matt's gaze softened. "I know that's right up your alley, which is why I'm approaching you."

Cole wasn't surprised his past was so well-known by complete strangers. "That's true. What did you have in mind? As much as I'd like to help, I don't have a lot of time."

"Actually, I think you're going to like what we've come up with. Some of the kids are interested in learning the contractor trade. I know you've got to need help to get the place fixed up on time, so I suggested the kids work with you after school and on

Saturdays. In exchange for their help, you show them the ropes of refinishing, some basic plumbing and electrical. Stuff like that."

Cole didn't know what to think. His knee-jerk reaction was to shy away. The kids would muck up the place, creating more work and slow the job down. He chastised himself. He'd prayed for help, and God had provided him with it. Sure it would probably be a ragtag group of teenagers that reminded him of himself at that age. If Dale Barrymore hadn't bailed Cole out and got him an internship in Phoenix, who knows where Cole would be today.

Everyone deserved the same break Cole had received. Renewed purpose energized him and filled him with gratitude, pushing away the darkness that had accompanied him to Dynamite Creek.

"I like the idea, but I can't use them right now. We're stripping lead paint and there are probably some asbestos hazards we haven't discovered yet. As long as Abby agrees though, I'll contact you when we're done with the demolition."

"Thanks for inviting me today." Abby stood in the refreshment line with Cole's sister while her daughter Nicole and another nine-year-old girl darted in and out of the waiting people. More kids, already sugared up on the sweets from the generous spread or food, played tag up and down the hallway outside, their echoes reverberating into the big room.

"You're welcome. As soon as we fill our plates, I'll introduce you to some of my friends." Christine shuffled ahead in line, giving Abby an unobstructed view of the rectangular room filled with three rows of long tables.

"I'd like that. The only people I know are my neighbors, one of the greeters and Cole's ex-partner, Robert."

"He's here?" The color fled from Christine's face, and her gaze darted around the room.

"He was, but he's already gone. He must have left the service early. Are you okay?"

Abby watched Christine take a huge breath and forced false laughter from her lips. "I'm fine. Really. I just can't believe he had the nerve to come back. Anyway, so what do you think of our humble church?"

Something seemed off in Christine's reaction and her words, but Abby took the other woman's lead and changed the subject. "I like it."

Abby meant every word. From the outer

brick walls, to welcoming foyer and the altar, a friendly atmosphere lingered everywhere. Even inside the community room. Colorful posters adorned the walls and a piano sat tucked in the corner opposite a big screen television. On another table, packets of organic coffee sat in boxes with a For Sale sign written in black marker on one of the flaps, as well as what looked like a cookbook. People of various ages occupied the banquet-style chairs and chatted among themselves or with others standing in line. The whole scene complemented the happy mood inside the church. Abby felt grounded, yet still inched up when the line moved a bit so she didn't stray too far from Christine, not that she wouldn't be able to spot her at a distance should they get separated.

Today Cole's sister wore a plain teal blue skirt with a white frilly blouse, but her oversized silver hoops, numerous bracelets and Concho necklace gave away her more artistic side. Despite the fact that two new inches of snow graced the ground from last night's storm, delicate tan and black cowboy boots encased her feet.

"I like your boots."

"Thanks. I got them over at a cowboy shop last time I was in Phoenix." Christine gave her a hesitant look, the kind that almost made Abby back up into the person behind her. "Cole mentioned you needed to go shopping for some things to go inside your house. I know some cute antique stores in Prescott if we can't find anything in Flagstaff. We could also venture into the Valley if you're game. Glendale has some great antique stores, too."

At the *S* word, her hunger disappeared. "Your brother told you I don't like to shop, hasn't he?"

Christine's merry laughter mingled with the clicking of her silver bracelets. "He mentioned it, but only because I dragged it out of him. Unlike me, he's not really a talker."

Abby dug the tip of her shoe into the square patterned carpet. Growing up an only child, Abby had no experience with sharing confidences with anyone other than her mother, and that ended way too soon. Their frequent moves had also made it impossible to establish close friendships, so most of the time she kept her emotions and thoughts bottled up inside. The few times she'd tried to reach out had ended in disaster with Abby the laughingstock of the classroom. Was she willing to take another chance? "It would probably take a lot longer than you'd have time for. I wouldn't want to put you out or anything."

Laying a warm hand on Abby's arm, Christine squeezed gently. "It would be my pleasure to show you around. If you'd like to join us for dinner tonight, I can show you a couple websites you can search that will give you some decorating ideas. When you narrow down the look you want, the shopping should be a breeze. Some of it can be done online, too."

"I'd like that." Hope blossomed at the sincerity of Christine's voice. Christine would be in town long after Cole disappeared and Abby wanted friendships that would span longer than a few months. Lifting her chin, Abby searched the room until she found Cole in discussion with the pastor over by the drinking fountain at the far end by the entrance. His gaze caught hers and the air sucked from her lungs. Feeling adrift and lost in a turbulent sea, Cole represented a safe harbor amid the chaos, despite his reaction to Robert.

"Dinner or the shopping?"

"Both. Thanks." Finally at the front of the buffet line, Abby set a piece of cinnamon coffee cake on the paper plate she'd grabbed, still uncertain about how God would or could play a role in her life.

Grapes found their way onto the plate followed by a few strawberries.

"You're welcome. I'll have Cole bring you over around four o'clock. We eat early on Sundays." Her bracelets jangled again as Christine filled a paper cup with orange juice.

They made their way to two empty chairs at one of the tables closest to the exterior wall. Introductions swirled around in Abby's head and faces and names blended together like milk in coffee.

Not hungry, but needing to do something with her fingers, Abby picked up a strawberry. Before she could take a bite, Christine waved the happy couple over. "Lauren. Julio. Over here."

"Abby, this is my best friend, Lauren Hamilton-Garza. Lauren, this is Abby Bancroft."

Abby dropped the fruit back down onto her plate and shook hands with the redheaded woman. "Pleased to meet you."

"You, too. Welcome to Dynamite Creek. This is my husband, Julio, and our darling daughter Gabriella. Gabby for short." The dark-haired, light olive skinned infant cooed in Lauren's arms and tried to grab the tiny gold cross suspended from her neck.

"She's beautiful. Congratulations." Wistfulness snuck into Abby's voice.

"Would you like to hold her while we grab something to eat?" Lauren held out the tiny infant.

Abby froze, her arms remaining at her sides. While Gabby was about the same size as Mittens, the tomcat didn't hold an air of fragility or helplessness. What if she dropped her, or held her wrong, or did something else?

"You won't hurt her. Babies aren't as fragile as people think." Christine took the baby first and shooed the parents away. "I remember when Nicole was this small." A pensive expression toyed with Christine's features. "Sometimes I wish —" Sadness pointed the corners of her lips to the floor. "Never mind. Nicole is so much easier now that she's in school. It was tough in the beginning."

Abby figured Christine was a single mom from the lack of a ring on her left hand, but her words just confirmed it. Where was Nicole's father? Apparently men walking away from their children were more commonplace than she'd realized.

Over the years, Abby had wondered about her father and in the beginning, she'd asked her mother until she grasped the futility of it. Mom would get a faraway look in her eyes and a bitter sadness consumed her for days, leaving Abby to fend for herself. After a while, she quit asking. Like Christine, Abby suspected her mother had done the best she could under the circumstances. A piece of resentment fell away, especially when Christine placed Gabby in Abby's arms.

The child was perfect. Abby sucked in a breath, unused to the weight and responsibility. As the seconds ticked by, Gabby settled down and stared up at her with big, blue eyes. For a moment, the air caught in her throat. Had her mom felt this way when she had held Abby in her arms?

Suddenly a maternal instinct broke free from all the layers of isolation. Her gaze met Cole's as he strode toward them and sucker punched her in the gut. What would a child of hers look like? What if Cole were the father? Would the baby look more like her or him? Green eyes or brown? Blond hair or brunette? Boy or girl? Heat seared her cheeks, yet she couldn't deny her attraction to the man.

The baby in her arms shifted, bringing Abby's attention back to the present. She dipped her head and her unbound hair swept across her face, giving her time to get her emotions in order before Cole reached her side.

"So, Cole, what do you think of our church?" Lauren moved the diaper bag off a chair and sat down. She held out her hands to take Gabby, much to Abby's relief.

Holding the baby brought out things best left alone until she got the bed-and-breakfast up and running and found someone willing to stick around.

"It's great. Everyone is very friendly and helpful." Abby didn't miss the tightness in his voice or the way he ran his fingers through his hair. Her shoulders tensed. She must have missed some inappropriate comment or stare. "Abby, may I have a word with you?"

"Sure. Are you ready to leave? We can discuss it on the way. We should get back to work you know." Abby half rose out of her seat before Cole motioned for her to sit down.

"No, we don't have to leave quite yet. I need to run something by you. Pastor Matt and his youth group want to help with the restoration."

"What? What's a youth group?" Abby wasn't sure she liked being talked about and having things decided for her but she kept her thoughts to herself until she learned more information.

Christine broke in to their conversation. "It's a group of teenagers that worship and hold Bible study here led by Pastor Matt. They go to fun activities like concerts, amusement parks, mini golf and stuff like that but it's so much more. It's a place where believers can hang out with other believers instead of running with the wrong crowd." His sister stared at Cole with sympathy. "They do a lot of humanitarian ministry, too, like food drives and mission trips. They're really awesome. Some of the girls came in to help me when I had a big order to fulfill last year on short notice."

"Cole, that's wonderful." Relaxing, Abby restrained herself from hugging him, which would surely cause tongues to start wagging. "That means we'll get done on time with the extra help." Her happiness sizzled like a used-up sparkler. "What's the catch? How much is it going to cost?"

Before Cole could answer, Abby's two neighbors marched up to their table. Dressed in their Sunday best flowery dresses, the formidable ladies flanked both sides and stared down at them.

"Abby and Cole must come to our house for dinner, I tell you. My pot roast is bigger."

"Now, Helen, we agreed it would be

mine." Betty huffed and crossed her arms across her ample chest. Her reading glasses hung suspended on a thin, colorfully beaded chain that broke the severity of her expression.

Abby's gaze ping-ponged between the two of them.

"But they've already agreed to come to my place for dinner." Christine stepped in between the two ladies this time. Abby pushed her chair as far away from the table as possible, only to be stopped by the wall.

"What's all this talk about food?" Another woman who'd introduced herself as Mrs. Campbell approached. Abby noticed her gaze trailed to the man standing beside her and they hardened a fraction. Interesting. Even inside the church some animosity remained.

"Since Abby and Cole are busy fixing up the Bancroft place, they don't have a lot of time to cook, so we're all talking turns inviting them over for dinner or making something and dropping it off. Which night would you like to host?"

"Speaking of hosting, we have a ladies' crafters club here on Monday nights and Bible study on Wednesdays. We'd love for you to join us when you're done with the house or need to get away for a bit," Alice

Henning, the pastor's wife, spoke up stepping in beside Helen.

Cole pulled the chair out next to Abby and sat down, his backbone stiff, his smile a little hardened around the edges. Abby could relate, but probably for different reasons. Being surrounded made her uncomfortable and she struggled for breath. She watched Cole pick up a grape from his sister's plate and roll it between his fingers. "What if Abby and I have other plans?"

Everyone including Abby turned and looked at Cole. Abby wondered if his reaction had to do with the few stares and whispers whirling around the room and the fact Abby had been invited to his sister's house. Still it would give her a chance to decline all the invitations, even if Cole had no plans at all.

"Yes, we do. Tell everyone about them," Abby managed to vocalize.

"I thought since we'd been working so hard on the place, we'd take the afternoon off and go do something fun and grab dinner afterward."

"You could go to the movies," Lauren spoke first as she adjusted the now sleeping Gabby in her arms.

Julio snapped his fingers. "How about bowling?"

"Go into Flagstaff," an elderly gentleman said from the table behind them, which started another heated discussion with the group of men.

"Meteor Crater isn't too far on the other side of Flagstaff either." Alice smiled.

"The Wupatki ruins are spectacular, too, if you're into Indian history." Betty sniffed. "You'll join us then for dinner tomorrow night?"

Nicole tugged on Cole's sleeve. "Why not go sledding, Uncle Cole? Miss Abby can use my sled and you can use my mom's. Then you can come by and eat dinner with us when you bring them back. Please? We're having homemade spaghetti tonight. My favorite."

The little girl's eyes grew round as she rubbed her belly, causing all the adults in the area to laugh.

After a few seconds, Cole placed his arm around Abby's shoulders and squeezed. "How can I say no to that? Spaghetti is my favorite, too. Sounds like a plan, don't you think?"

"This is it?" Abby stared at Watson Hill ten miles to the west of Flagstaff, her eyes widening after Cole pulled into the last vacant parking space and shut off the engine. Her gloved hands twisted together. The image of broken arms and legs danced before her vision.

"Yep. It hasn't changed much since I was a kid." Cole pulled a knitted black cap over his hair and gave her another one of his famous grins that set her heartbeat at top speed. This effect he had on her had to stop or she'd be a dried-up husk of skin and bones by the time he left, if there were any body parts remaining after this afternoon.

"But it's not a hill, it's the side of a mountain." She thought twice about sitting on a slick piece of plastic and speeding down *the hill,* but in comparison to the risks at sitting close to Cole, she was probably safer among the bumps in the snow. Through the windshield, Abby watched a preteen boy careen down the hill, go airborne, and then plow into another teen at the bottom. Her stomach took up residence in the borrowed snow boots.

"You've never sledded before, have you?"

Abby shook her head. "On second thought, don't you think we should go back and work on the house? We are on a time crunch."

"I think we're entitled to a few hours off. I'll work late tomorrow night. Come on, it's fun." After jumping from the driver's seat and marching around the front end, he opened her door and held out his hand. "I'll go down with you the first time."

Somehow Abby found herself on the outside of Cole's truck, her hand inside his. Even though they both wore gloves, Abby still felt his warmth. She wasn't so sure sledding was a great idea as they trudged through the snow, Cole dragging the plastic sleds behind them. Fifteen miles north and east of town the six new inches of snow sucked at her boots and glistened in the sunlight. While Cole practically danced through the new accumulation, it reminded Abby of trying to run a marathon through sand dunes. A pang of homesickness welled inside. Instead of palm trees, she had pines. Instead of sand, she had snow. Instead of brick and stucco, she had a monstrous Victorian that still needed a ton of work.

At least it was hers. Finally, a real place to call home.

When Cole wedged the smaller sled against a tree at the top of the gently rising hill, she shook off her melancholy mood. Abby had other things to worry about right now. Her knees threatened to buckle. From the bottom, the run hadn't looked that bad, but from her vantage point now, it took her breath away and unleashed a gaggle of butterflies inside her stomach. No matter how much she tried to convince herself this would be like another day at the beach, she failed miserably. The beach she understood, the mountains daunted her.

"We'll do the bunny hill first so you get a feel for it." His arm tucked through hers, he led her to the smallest slope filled with younger kids. From farther up the hill, screams and laughter echoed in her ears while a kaleidoscope of color from jackets, scarves and hats filled her vision. The scent of pine carried over on the light, but crisp wind, which stung the exposed skin on her face. Sunlight reflected in the white snow and continued to melt the accumulation clinging to the tree branches. A few rocks poked out near the edges of the runs and on the more popular runs, a light layer of ice had been uncovered by the early morning sledders.

"You first." Cole held the sled so it wouldn't rush down the hill without them.

Once Abby settled herself in the front part, Cole positioned himself behind her, the sled dipping under his weight. He sat way too close but there was no more room in the hard plastic. Abby had wedged herself as far forward as possible. She wondered if the weight would slow them down, or make them go faster. Preferably the former but with her luck it would be the latter. His arm wrapped around her waist as he tucked his legs next to hers in the bright red sled, creating a tiny sense of security.

His warm breath tickled her ear lobe, sending a delicious wave of awareness through her. "Ready?"

Abby nodded, unsure if the turbulence in her stomach had anything to do with the impending ride. The bottom of the hill looked like a huge sled-eating monster, waiting to engulf them in its cold embrace.

Cole pushed the sled forward until it tilted downward and let gravity do the rest of the work. The plastic sailed over the snow as they sped toward the bottom of the hill. Wind whipped her hair in her face and stung her cheeks. Caged butterflies whirled around in her stomach at the quick descent. A few tiny bumps interrupted the smooth ride, until finally the sled came to rest at the bottom. Laughter trickled from Abby's lips as she allowed Cole to pull her up.

"Well, what do you think?"

A huge smile emerged from behind her cold lips. She hadn't had that much fun in years. "That was awesome."

"Ready to try it by yourself?"

Abby watched a toddler speed by, the little

pompom on her pink cap bobbing up and down in the wind. Her shrieks and the terrified look on her pale face as she sailed past caused a blip in Abby's happy mood. Sledding wasn't a sport for the faint at heart, and she would be lying if she said she didn't like the feel of Cole's arms wrapped around her. "No. I'm sure the other sled will be okay against the tree, won't it?"

"No problem."

Thirty minutes later and seven runs down the intermediate hill, Abby finally gained enough confidence to try the advanced run. Sitting at the top of the slope though, even with the benefit of Cole's warmth, she questioned her sanity. The downward slope stared back at her as if daring her to take the plunge. She inhaled deeply, taking in another breath of fresh mountain-pine-laden air. Gently, Cole rocked the sled back and forth to gain momentum to propel them down the hill. "Three, two, one."

A quarter of the way down, wind continued to whip Abby's hair into her eyes and nipped at her nose. Her hands gripped the useless rope because the sled had a mind of its own as it careened down the hill. A huge bump loomed in front of them and within seconds they were airborne. A scream split her lips and she closed her eyes, waiting for the imminent collision. After the sled crashed back down on the snow and dumped them out and over the side, cold enfolded her in its icy embrace. The impact forced the air from her lungs and she slid sideways, finally coming to rest against a small tree stump off the path.

Face up Abby tentatively wiggled her fingers and toes. No pain. Then she moved her arms and legs. Still nothing. She shifted on the cold snow. Good. Nothing broken or injured. How had Cole fared? Her heart slammed in her chest and her lungs cried out for air. If he'd hurt himself . . . She turned her head and caught movement in the figure sprawled out beside her. If she wasn't mistaken, she thought she heard muffled laughter. "Cole?"

"That didn't go as planned. Are you okay?" Cole rolled over until only a few inches separated them and stared down at her, a smile twitching his lips. Snow covered his hat, his eyelashes and a few flakes clung to his exposed hair. More melted snow trickled down his cheek. Abby saw the tension fall away in his unguarded expression and she captured the moment to remember for years to come.

He wedged his elbow into the snow and rested his head against his palm. His other hand gently brushed away the moisture from her cheek. Abby didn't feel the cold anymore, only the path of warmth left by his gloved fingers. With his sunglasses lost in the crash, she watched the color of his eyes deepen to a delicious shade of dark chocolate as he dipped his head closer. His lips hovered a fraction above hers and it was all she could do not to reach up and wrap her arms around his neck and pull him down to satisfy her question of how it would feel to kiss Cole.

She was falling in love, which would only lead to more heartache and pain. Tearing her gaze from his, she stared up at the blue sky and laughed at her own stupidity and to break the connection between them. "I'm fine. Next time you steer."

The spell broken, he jumped to his feet before helping her up. "You're willing to do it again?"

"Of course. I've had worse moments bodysurfing." Abby dusted the snow from her jacket and jeans.

"Bodysurfing?"

"When I wasn't working, I didn't sit around working on a tan. I couldn't afford a surfboard and boogie boarding wasn't my style."

"Interesting. What did you do?"

"I was a lifeguard for a few years in high school." At his questioning look, Abby raised her hand to stop the stream of questions she knew were on the tip of his tongue. "It was nothing glamorous like that TV show. Most days, I sat around in the chair counting the number of one-piece suits versus bikinis and blowing an occasional whistle at kids with more brawn than brains."

"And after that?" Cole collected the sled and his sunglasses and they began the trudge back up the side of the hill. He reached out and grabbed her hand as if it were the most natural thing in the world. Abby didn't resist, liking the idea that they looked like a couple even though she knew it was the furthest thing from Cole's mind.

"I wanted to go to college and get a degree in business."

"What stopped you?"

"My mother died and I had a hard time accepting it. After that, I drifted around in a bunch of dead-end jobs until I came here."

Cole stopped midway up the hill and turned to face her. He pushed a stray curl behind her ear, his warm breath fanned her face again as he leaned closer and cupped her face with his gloved hands. A few teenagers jostled by and gave them a smirk but Abby ignored them. She'd had a lot of practice.

"I'm really sorry about that, Abby. I know words hardly compare to your loss, but if you share your burden with God, it will lessen your pain. I didn't go through a death of a loved one, but in a way I lost my mom, too, and I experienced the death of a business and the trust of a person I'd admired. God helped me through those days. I know He can help you, too, if you'd let Him."

Abby's eyelids fluttered down to avoid the compassion and belief written in Cole's eyes. She shifted in the snow and felt the weight of his gaze drag her under in its current. She floundered in both the weather and the emotions swirling around her. Something had started to change in her today inside that church. Something she couldn't quite describe but she finally felt like she was going in a positive direction. "I'll think about it, Cole. Really, I will. I did go today and I enjoyed myself. That was a beginning. Race you to the top?"

After another thirty minutes of sledding, Cole lowered the tailgate and spread out a multicolored Mexican blanket. Satisfied that Abby would be comfortable, he wrapped his hands around her waist and lifted her up. He liked the way she felt in his arms even though he could feel the bones in her hips through her jeans. When Abby pulled her hands from his shoulders, a sense of loss surrounded him, yet he took his cue from her. He retreated inside the cab of his truck, pulled out two cups and the thermos and then walked to where she sat.

After pouring out the steaming hot chocolate, he picked up his own drink and leaned against the back of his truck, not trusting himself to sit next to her. Today he'd seen another side to Abby. A not-so-serious side that broke past her defenses and chased away her ever-present sadness. "I don't know about you, but I'm glad you're here."

"Me, too. Thanks to Nicole's suggestion." When she smiled, tiny dimples appeared at the corners of her mouth. Red tinted the tip of her nose and added a healthy glow to her cheeks. She gently blew across the foamy brown surface before taking a sip.

"So am I."

"Maybe we could do it again sometime?"

"Maybe." Taking the cup from her, he set both his and hers down on the blanket and lowered his head.

He knew he shouldn't, yet he still did, drawn in by the promise of Abby's lips. They were just as soft and sweet as he'd imagined they would be, and now her breath hinted of chocolate and ice. In that one simple caress, he tried to convey the mixed-up feelings he had for her and as she responded, he tried to think of every reason why he shouldn't be kissing Abby Bancroft. Like her lack of belief in God and her decision to let Robert in the house and the broken trust it caused. It didn't matter as much now because despite his opinion about the Robert issue, she had attended church with him today. He found himself falling for Abby.

Maybe he didn't have to leave when he finished fixing up her house.

CHAPTER NINE

"Now it's time to have some fun." Christine's arms dipped under the stack of photo albums she'd retrieved from the bookcase next to the fireplace. After placing them on the wood floor by Abby's feet, she stepped over Cole's outstretched ones, walked around the dark brown sofa and stood behind their mother while their stepfather sat in the matching chair. Cole's niece perched herself on the other side and wrapped her arm around Annette's shoulders.

Cole knew what his sister was trying to do and he suspected Abby did too when her hand immediately found his. Maybe the old photos would trigger something in his mother's mind that would bring back the memories of him. That's what he got for leaving Dynamite Creek and remaining a stranger to his own family. His gaze searched the puzzled expression on his mother's face and his grip tightened on Abby's.

Self-loathing ripped a fresh hole in his emotions. If only he'd been there when the accident occurred maybe he could have done something. Anything. But he'd been living in Phoenix, trying to put his past behind him, working to make a name for himself, and finding God.

Years later, his path led him back home. It had to be part of God's plan. But was Abby included in that? Or was she just another person in his life to help him grow? Her hand fit well in his and they shared some similar interests. The remembered feel of her lips and how well she responded to him earlier sent his blood careening through his veins and he found himself wanting to kiss her again like he had after sledding.

The situation was only temporary, and he had no right to raise any hope in Abby that there could be anything between them. He'd left the small town in disgrace because he'd made one huge mistake in his teens.

How had that affected his mother? In his selfishness, Cole hadn't even considered how his actions hurt those he loved. And now he could place Abby in that category. He released her hand and instantly felt lost and sad. Making the break now though would only benefit them in the long run when he returned to Phoenix.

Christine grabbed the top album and flipped open the first page. Her laughter filled the small area. "Okay then, here we are as infants. I'm the cute one on the right, Abby."

As if Abby wouldn't be able to tell the difference. Despite the pink bow that wrapped around Christine's fuzzy head and the softer features, as infants they looked very similar even though they were fraternal twins. Yet Christine held a fragile air around her, and Cole had always protected his sister growing up. His gaze shot to Nicole. Except that one time, but his sister's rebellion had taken place when she'd been an adult and had come to stay with him in Phoenix for several months. He still didn't know who the father was, and each time he'd asked, Christine's lips sealed tight.

He glanced down at the photos again, this time at their first birthday party. Dark hair replaced the peach fuzz, their eyes had changed from blue to brown and they'd each started growing into their own distinct features. A cone hat sat perched on his head and frozen in time, Cole's pudgy hand grabbed for it, as if trying to pull it off. A few photographs later, Cole wore most of his birthday cake on his face and hands and had smeared the rest on Christine. Heat seared his cheeks. If he didn't love his sister, he'd kill her right about now.

"How cute." Cole heard the longing in Abby's voice. "I wish my mom had taken more photos of me when I was younger. I think she bought into the theory that photographs took a piece of your soul."

Cole fell into Abby's pained expression and his grip instinctively wrapped around her waist as if to shield her from her memories. Twisting at the waist, he faced her and reached out to tuck a stray curl behind her ear. It was all he could do not to kiss the sorrow from her lips and the sadness from her eyes. Surrounded by family though, he couldn't act on the impulse as his fingers trailed down the soft contours of her cheek before dropping them into his lap. "Who knows? You moved around so much, they might have been left behind by accident."

"Maybe." A hesitant smile lit her lips. "At least I don't have any blackmail pictures lying around."

Cole groaned, knowing Abby referred to the photo when he was three and washing his ride-n-style yellow and red car covered in nothing but mud and a pair of superman shorts.

"I knew that would get Cole in trouble

some day." His mother coughed and his stepfather immediately put a hand on her back. A flash of recognition flared before the blank mask descended again. His mom glanced at her husband. "Manny, did we ever have any children?"

"No, *mija.* But you have two beautiful children and a granddaughter right over there."

"I do, don't I? I'm so lucky."

God had blessed his mom with Manny. Would He do the same with Cole?

When Abby rested her head against his shoulder, he wondered what it would be like to spend the rest of his life with her. No! He had to stop thinking of a future with Abby. His parents hadn't gotten it right the first time, what made him think he could?

"Oh look, here we are on our first day of school." Christine continued to flip the pages. "And here's you with your first fish."

Cole stiffened. Behind the smiling boy staring back at him, a man stood with his hands on his shoulders. His father. The fishing trip had been the last time they'd been together as father and son. Pain ripped through his heart and deep down he blamed himself for the defection. If he'd been a better son, maybe his father wouldn't have left.

"Remember when we used to catch fireflies and put them in a jar in our rooms to use as night-lights?" Christine changed the subject as if detecting his thoughts.

"And how you cried when they were all dead in the morning?" Like the part of him that cried out for a father who'd abandoned his family.

Five photo albums later, the pictures stopped at their high school graduation. Cole looked good in his black cap and gown, yet behind the smile, he saw the ache reflected in his eyes again. While he stared at the camera, he looked beyond the photographer, searching for his father, who didn't even have the decency to show up.

"Time to go, Abby. We've got a lot to do tomorrow." He quickly shut the album and set it back down by his feet. Cole buried his grief behind the wall Abby had managed to breach, determined to resurrect it again and mentally pulled away from her.

Abby deserved someone who would stay around.

While Abby was out for her jog Monday morning, Cole glanced out the dining room window as Robert dragged the stepladder underneath the ceiling damage. Tension hung between them because there was so much unsaid, yet Cole couldn't find the strength to bring up the subject. When Robert was ready to talk about it, if ever, he'd have to be the one to bring up the discussion.

Cole's fingers dusted some of the residue from the newly stripped windowsill as soft sunlight filtered into the room, bringing out just how much work still lay ahead of them. At this rate, if they got the main floor done and the two bedrooms Abby had rented out completed by the Founder's Day Festival, it would be amazing, but he wouldn't be happy until he'd finished the project. The sooner the better because after yesterday, he realized he was falling for his temporary boss.

Turning away from the early signs of spring unfolding on the other side of the glass, Cole focused on his ex-partner. Contrasting against the earthy green, Robert's pale skin stretched across his features and his work clothes hung from his body as if they were meant for someone else. Shadows clung to the delicate area beneath his eyes and a brittle air surrounded him.

Even though they'd worked together before they formed their partnership ten years earlier, there was so much about Robert he didn't know. Like himself, Robert had gotten into trouble in his teens, but he'd never spoken of it. He'd never talked about his early life or where he disappeared to on the weekends until Cole had found out about his gambling addiction, but he'd always been a hard worker until the end.

In Cole's haste to make it on his own so he could hold up his head and put his past behind him, he hadn't thought to see if Robert's visions matched his own. A mistake he wouldn't make again once he was back on his feet. On the few occasions when he'd returned to Dynamite Creek to see his mom and sister, instead of a welcome, he had felt the stares of the townspeople who labeled him as the troubled youth. Some of them still did.

Would fixing up the Bancroft house really change people's opinions of him or was he just fooling himself? The answer didn't fill him with much confidence as he eyed Robert. A burning sensation stung the back of his neck at the way his ex-partner's gaze skittered away and returned to stare at the damaged ceiling above him.

Cole followed his lead. "Do you think it's worth replacing or should we go with drywall?"

"I can fix it but it's going to take awhile. So is fixing the wall in the parlor. At least the leak was fixed years ago, but it might be in Abby's best interests to have a plumber come check everything. Not my area of expertise."

"Mine either. I'm glad you agree. I met just the person for the job at church yesterday. As long as Abby approves, I'll give him a call."

"Sounds good. I like that church."

"Me, too." Cole donned his work gloves and flexed his fingers. They didn't have time to stand around. Maybe once they'd gotten further along, they'd have more time to clear the air.

"I like how everyone is so nice and helpful. I wish those kids could come in right now. It would sure speed things along."

"Yeah, but we wouldn't want one of them to get sick and have that hanging over our heads. Asbestos and lead are pretty serious stuff."

"Point taken. Look —" Robert walked over to him, ran a hand along his unshaven jaw, his expression taut, his eyes trying to convey some meaning Cole didn't understand. "Never mind."

They'd never really talked before about anything unrelated to business. Cole didn't want to start now. Not while he still felt the sting of his ex-partner's defection and betrayal. He picked up his water he'd brought from the kitchen and drained the glass, while the uncomfortable silence stretched between them, threatening to shatter the fragile truce. Robert turned away, climbed up on the stepladder and ran his fingers along the upper edge of the wall. Plaster flaked down on his head and shoulders.

"I'm not going to be able to salvage the mural which is a shame. The artisan quality is the best I've seen in a long time." Robert jumped down and planted his back end on the top step. His stare made Cole shift his weight. "You like Abby, don't you?"

Cole almost dropped the glass. He stepped back, messing up the drop cloth and knocking over the bucket used to collect the stripped paint. His arms flailed before he managed to catch his balance. Avoiding Robert's gaze, he righted the bucket and smoothed out the cloth with his feet. "I don't see how liking Abby has anything to do with fixing plaster."

"It doesn't, and I do think you like her and she likes you. I can see it in the way you two look at each other. Don't make the same mistake I did."

"And what mistake would that be?" Scraping a hand through his hair, Cole paced the confines of the empty dining room. Concern and confusion wracked his emotions and churned the coffee he'd drunk earlier that morning. Cole counted ten paces, turned counted five, turned and paced another few steps. The room crowded in, the four bare walls where he and Abby had peeled away the five layers of wallpaper mocked him.

"Aside from financially ruining the one friend I had, years ago I hurt the woman I loved deeply because I couldn't handle my emotions. Like you, I left her before she could reject me. I can only hope she'll take me back when I finally get to talk to her."

"What made you change?" Cole didn't understand the regret and self-loathing that flashed across Robert's features.

"Jail time and the preacher who rescued me while I was in there." Robert reached for his own water glass, took a drink, and then rubbed his mouth with the back of his hand. "Don't leave Abby like you've done with everyone. You've got to let somebody love you or you'll be alone the rest of your life. That's not what I want. It's not what you want either."

"No. It's not." But Cole didn't want to be trapped in a loveless relationship, either. Floorboards creaked under his paint-splattered tan work boots as he continued to pace. He tugged at the neck of his faded

T-shirt, Robert's voice echoing in his brain. If he took the time to analyze his ex-partner's words, he knew he'd see the truth. In his own way, he'd repeated his father's footsteps, most of the time leaving before he got too involved, a few times being left and confirming the pattern he'd learned as a youth.

Robert's appearance back in Dynamite Creek turned everything upside down and left Cole more confused than ever.

Taking a break from ripping up the carpet in the living room Monday midafternoon, Abby stared at the piece of paper in her hand that had come in the day's mail. A Chamber of Commerce Potluck? Saturday? Her grip tightened, the sound of crinkling paper echoing in her ears. She reread the words and squeezed her eyelids shut, but nothing could block out the words that blazed inside her skull like a neon beacon in the darkness. *Bring a dish to share.*

Dragging in a ragged breath, she opened her eyes and released the flyer, but not before she became the proud owner of a paper cut on her pinkie. The paper fluttered to the table. Dampness coated her palms and the ever-present butterflies grew active again in her stomach as she smoothed out the wrinkled pale yellow paper. The multi-colored words and pictures sprinkled across the sheet spelled acceptance even though her B and B hadn't technically opened for business yet.

She thought about her two neighbors Helen and Betty and how they contrasted each other, but each of them knew how to cook. Abby shook her head to dispel the images of fires and other cooking disasters. She could do this. If she could take on the job of helping to renovate a thirteen-plus-room Victorian, she could certainly come up with something to bring to the potluck — like her grandmother's infamous blueberry scone recipe. Her future guests the Gordons had specifically requested them, so she'd better figure out sooner rather than later how to make them.

Retying the bandanna around her head, she strode to the pantry and stared at the almost empty shelves. A few cans of beans, tomato sauce, fruits and vegetables, and a bag of cat food occupied the lowest shelf and a brand-spanking-new set of spices sat on the eye level one. She'd also picked up some spaghetti sauce and noodles along with some prepackaged box meals when she'd gone to the store, but mostly she and Cole either carried in or scavenged through the refrigerator when they weren't eating dinner at someone else's house. "At least I won't have any trouble replacing the contact paper before I fully stock. So, if I were a recipe, where would I be?"

Abby left the pantry and kicked the door shut behind her. She rechecked all the white cabinets in the small kitchen, some of them sticking because of all the layers of paint. "Slim pickings here."

Once this place was up and running and she finally made some money, Abby would consider Cole's idea of expanding into the mudroom and replacing the late sixties theme with something a little more modern, which also included adding a dishwasher and disposal. A new refrigerator and stove would also be nice, especially since the antiquated stove seemed to have a mind of its own as to when it wanted to work.

Stepping through the entryway into the mudroom, Abby almost tripped over a sleeping Mittens curled on the rug by the back door. The tomcat jumped up and then stretched his black and white paws and put his rear end in the air. A huge yawn showed his sharp fangs and dark, pink tongue. "Sorry, buddy." Abby opened the back door, letting the warmer breezes of the coming spring inside the small room. "Out you go. Now don't go bothering Fifi, you hear?"

Once the cat disappeared underneath the hedge dividing the properties, Abby shut the door and spun around. She faced the old stained cabinet obviously added as an afterthought, suspended above the wooden bench where her grandmother's gardening boots still sat along with a pair of yellow gloves.

"Can't hurt to look."

When she pulled open the doors, she spied rows of cookbooks perched on the three shelves. "Yes."

Grabbing an armful, she traipsed back to the kitchen table and began her search. Two glasses of iced tea and eight cookbooks later, frustration pecked at the confidence she'd gained when she'd discovered the cache of books. Her fingers drummed the Formica surface.

"Abby? What are you doing?" Cole stuck his head through the doorway. White flakes dusted his hair and clothing, while carpet fibers clung to his painters pants. Fatigue toyed with the delicate skin under his eyes and deepened the lines creasing his forehead.

"I found my grandmother's cookbooks. I'm looking for her blueberry scone recipe to make and bring to the Chamber of Commerce potluck on Saturday." She pushed the invitation across the table's surface.

Striding over, Cole picked up the flyer. "Potluck?"

Even though she didn't want to feel anything for him, her heartbeat accelerated at his nearness and her mouth went dry. His masculine scent tickled her nose each time she dragged in a ragged breath. "Yes."

"That will be a good way to meet the prominent people."

"I know. That's what I was thinking." She flipped open a three-ring binder filled with plastic sheets and rifled through recipes cut out from magazines and newspapers and handwritten ones on thin white paper. "Would you like to come with me?"

She glanced up in time to see the corners of Cole's mouth turn south and distance cloud his brown eyes. His nostrils flared and the whiteness of his knuckles gleamed against his tanned skin. "No, thanks. Christine should be there though. She can keep you company."

"Okay." Disappointed, she flipped to the back of the binder and a few loose pieces of paper spilled out with her grandmother's flowery handwriting. *Finally.* The recipe she'd spent the good part of the last hour looking for. She pulled out the elusive sheet and ran her fingers over the loops and swirls. The faint scent of lavender wrapped around her, comforting her.

"You never did tell me what my grandmother was like. I picture a plump woman with blue hair worn back in a bun and one of those granny smocks the elderly are known for. Kind of like a cross between Helen and Betty."

Cole's laughter filled the room. "Far from it. Don't let her handwriting deceive you. She was thin, wore trendy clothes and styled her hair in the latest fashion. She had a tough side to her because of your grandfather, but she always had a soft side for us kids. Or at least she was like that before I left. I didn't see her after I quit shoveling their walk and driveway."

"It would have been nice to have met her." The recipe blurred before her as silence chilled the interior that Abby wasn't sure the radiator heat could ever chase away. In her own selfishness, she'd reminded Cole that because of Robert's theft, the town still blamed Cole for the Bancrofts' deaths. "I'm sorry. You must have come in to find me for something."

"I've encountered another problem I need you to see." The professional side to Cole returned.

Abby was only too glad to straighten out her neck and leave the cookbooks and the images Cole's words conjured up behind her. At least she'd found her recipe and could plan a trip to the grocery store to get the supplies by Friday. The steps creaked under their weight and the unfinished wood railing felt rough beneath her palm because they'd decided to save all the varnishing, painting and wallpapering until the end when the youth group could come in and help.

"What is it?" She followed him into the master bedroom.

"While I was pulling down the paneling in here, I discovered a fireplace hidden behind a few of the panels."

"That's good news, isn't it?" Abby scratched the back of her head. "And if this room had one, don't you think the others on this floor might, too?"

"Probably and yes, I guess you could consider it good news, from an esthetic point of view but not a practical one. Look." Cole motioned for her to stick her head inside the fireplace.

Abby stared down the hole and saw the bottom of the parlor fireplace. Her stomach landed next to the hearth on the first floor.

"You won't be able to use either one unless we reconfigure everything."

Abby pulled her head out and sat back on her heels. Her fingers gripped her knees. "Why not?"

"Smoke inhalation. You'd probably kill your guests." Cole joined Abby on the faded throw rug as a ghost of a smile crept to his lips. "Not exactly the type of reputation you want to have."

"No. That could put a damper on things. What are you thinking of doing?"

"The easiest thing would be to seal it up, but I have to admit that a fireplace adds a charm you just can't find these days. So, with that in mind, I've got to figure a way to get the smoke to bypass this room and then reconstruct the fireplace back to its original state."

"That's probably going to take a while." Another setback. More frustration curled around her heart. Three steps forward always resulted in at least one step back.

"What does that mean?" Abby's confidence deflated early Saturday afternoon as she stared at her grandmother's handwritten recipe. She'd mixed together all the dry ingredients just like it said, but the next instructions baffled her. "Cut in the butter?"

Leaving the bowl on the counter, she paced the floor. "Where's the *Cooking for Dummies* book when I need one? Cut in butter. Cut in butter. Okay, I can figure this out."

She stalked back to the counter and grabbed the knife she'd used to cut the stick into smaller pieces. Wielding the utensil like a pick, she stabbed at one of the many cubes of butter sitting in on top of the flour mixture. The clump stuck to the knife and refused to drop off. She thrust the blade back into the mixture.

"Hi, Abby. I'm back from the workshop. What are you doing?" Cole's voice held a trace of amusement and confusion as he entered the kitchen.

"I'm trying to make blueberry scones." Abby's spine stiffened until the tension created an instant headache. Dropping the knife, she placed her hands on her hips and turned to face him.

"By killing the batter?" Cole turned on the faucet and put his glass underneath.

"Sure. Can't think of any other way to cut in butter, can you?"

When Cole took a long drink, she couldn't help but notice the strong column of his neck or the way his fingers so tenderly cradled the fragile glass. The same fingers that had held hers several times and had offered comfort when she'd needed it. After he set the glass on the counter opposite where Abby had placed the bowl, his footsteps ate up the short distance between them, causing another hitch in her breathing. The man looked more comfortable in her kitchen and the entire house than she did.

"Sometimes cookbooks have glossaries or techniques listed in the back, but I can help you on this one. You need two knives or a pastry blender. I bet your grandmother had one around here somewhere." He pulled out the first drawer, saw silverware and pushed it shut. The second drawer garnered the same fate. He yanked out the third one and rummaged through the contents, finally pulling out a wicked looking U-shaped tool with five bowed blades at the bottom and attached together by a metal handle. "Voilà! Pastry blender."

After washing his hands, he grabbed the bowl, plunged the tool into the butter and began to cut the chunks into smaller pieces. Abby leaned against the counter and watched his muscles flex as he repeatedly punched the cutter into the bowl until the mixture resembled coarse crumbs. She could never grow tired of seeing Cole inside her home and tucked away the memory.

He set the bowl down and tapped the remnants clinging to the pastry blender back into the mixture before he sifted some of the contents. "What's next?"

Cole gave her another one of his grins that sent her emotions ducking for cover behind her own glass of water. The kitchen area had shrunk to the size of the pantry with Cole's presence, and yet he showed no signs of leaving.

Abby picked up the recipe and read the next sentence, only too glad to put the piece of paper between her line of vision and Cole. "It says to make a well in the center and pour in the cream, then fold together but don't overwork the dough, whatever that means."

She watched him scoop out the center with a spoon and spread the contents equally around the sides. Then he picked up the measuring glass and container of cream. "It means that you want to mix the batter until everything sticks together. Overworking it will make the scones tough. How much cream?"

"One cup. Where'd you learn how to do all this?"

"My mom." He measured and poured the cream and then his hands worked magic.

Within minutes, Cole formed a ball inside the bowl. "She loved to cook and passed that love down to me. I think she also wanted to make sure Christine and I could fend for ourselves. She had a hard time adjusting when my dad split, so she made sure we knew a little about everything. I haven't spent much time in the kitchen lately though. There's been no reason."

"Maybe that will change when you finish here and figure out where you want to go next." The thought of Cole's departing produced a pain in her heart. Until then, she'd enjoy his company and learn as much as she could about repairing and keeping up the old house and cooking as it turned out.

"How many blueberries?"

"One cup."

Cole rinsed the blueberries, measured them and dumped them on top of the ball of dough. "The trick is not to mash or bruise these things or they'll bleed."

"So, you love old houses, you're a pro on a sled and a chef in the kitchen. What other deep, dark secrets are you hiding?"

"I love watching the Food Channel." Cole knew enough about baking and eating and, for that matter, he knew where to go from here without looking at the recipe. He sprinkled flour across the surface of the wood cutting board and dumped out the dough.

"The Food Channel? Really? That surprises me. I would have thought one of the home shows would be more your style."

"Oh, I like those, too, but cooking is so basic and simple, and it doesn't take months to see the results." Food also brought him comfort and he'd found it was the one thing he could control. He rummaged through the bottom drawer again and pulled out a rolling pin. He stepped back, handed it to Abby, and then guided her into place in front of him. "Since these are your grandmother's specialties, you'd better know how to make them."

Her sigh squeezed the blood from his heart and he wished he could erase the tension riveting her spine into an unbendable steel rod. "You can do this, Abby. If you can operate a paint remover, strip wallpaper and tear out carpet, you can master an itty, bitty scone."

Cole placed his hands over hers and guided her movements until the dough formed a rectangle. Her hands were so soft and smooth under his callouses and the sensation of holding her in his arms wreaked havoc with his will to leave. He shouldn't torment himself and yet all he wanted to do was bury his nose in the floral scent of her silky hair and kiss the patch of exposed skin at the base of her neck. He leaned in, trying to absorb her warmth to chase away the chill that had descended over him.

Abby deserved better than a punk vandal, a wild child, a man who let his ex-partner dupe a prominent senior couple out of thousands. He knew that staying around could jeopardize her continued acceptance in Dynamite Creek. He wouldn't be responsible for more loss in Abby's life. His lips barely skimmed the crown of her head before he pulled back.

"You're going to want to cut this into small triangles because I suspect there's going to be a lot of people there. I'll be back upstairs if you need me." Cole retreated before he did anything else foolish.

CHAPTER TEN

Sitting in her office doing internet research, Abby smelled something burning. "My scones!" She shoved back the chair and flew from the room. "What happened to my timer?"

That would teach her to pay attention to what she was doing. Multitasking might work well for some, but not someone trying to do a full remodel at the same time. She'd gotten lost in a website that sold authentic historical silk wallpaper and either hadn't heard the timer or had never checked to see that it worked properly.

It didn't matter at this second if she'd found the perfect cream and pale green print with stars and fleurs-de-lis for the parlor. If she didn't pull off a good impression on the chamber people, her bed-and-breakfast would sizzle like the scones inside her oven.

She pulled out the first cookie sheet and

dumped it on top of the stove. Tears burned at the back of her eyes. Her contribution to the Dynamite Creek Chamber of Commerce potluck wouldn't win her any friends or business acquaintances.

"Are the scones burning?" Abby turned and watched Cole enter the kitchen again with a paint scraper still in his hand. Flecks of old paint sprinkled his face, his baseball cap and the uncovered parts of his hair. More removed paint splattered on his T-shirt and a finger mark stood out where he'd wiped his hands on his painters pants.

"They're ruined. I'm sorry." Abby hated the feeling of inadequacy as she faced the oven again, pulled out the second cookie sheet and put it next to the first. She threw down the pot holder. It shouldn't matter what the people thought of her. She'd outgrown that before she hit her teens. Or at least she thought she did.

He moved in behind her, spun her around to face him and put his hand on her shoulders. "They're just scones, Abby."

"I know but I wanted to make a good impression. I wanted everything to be perfect. My grandmother's reputation is proving harder to live up to than I'd anticipated." Abby wiped away the errant tear from her cheek.

Cole gathered her close and wrapped his arms around her waist. He rested his chin on top of her head while his fingers massaged the small of her back. "Is the house burning?"

Abby absorbed the comfort he offered and shook her head. The steady beating of his heart thrummed in her ears and she relished the closeness she felt with Cole.

"Has something happened to Mittens? Or maybe someone else you care about?"

"No."

"Look at me, Abby." He tilted her head back so she had no choice but to lose herself in the depths of his eyes. "Things can be replaced. People and pets can't. Burning your scones is not the end of the world, no matter how it seems right now."

His lips were mere inches away. The remembered feel of them on hers after sledding scared away her ability to breathe. Seconds that lasted an eternity buzzed between them as his gaze lingered on her. Her eyes closed milliseconds before Cole's mouth claimed hers. His caress chased away the loneliness in her life. She felt his strength as her arms wrapped around his neck and pulled him closer. Her lips sought his, pouring out her emotions to him through the connection because she was unable to vocalize the feelings he released.

She loved him, which changed everything between them. She couldn't go back to the boss-employee relationship.

He raised his head and blinked. The moment disappeared, yet he lifted his hand and trailed his knuckles down her cheek. A look of regret chased away the lingering promise of the kiss.

"Don't get any ideas, Abby. I'm not the permanent kind of guy you're looking for."

Of course not. Cole had found it necessary to remind her that his time was only temporary and in a few weeks, he'd be gone.

Abby hid her hurt behind the wall she'd developed as a child. She could change her surroundings, but she couldn't change the disappointment that seemed to follow her. "I know that. The only idea I have right now is to come up with another contribution to the potluck."

All business again, Cole washed his hands. He slung the towel over his shoulder and thrust his hands out in front of him, cracking his knuckles. "If you take a seat, I'll start over again or whip something else up."

"I can't let you make something else for me, I was supposed to make it."

"The invitation said *bring a dish to share.* I saw nothing about you having to be the

245

one to make it. I bet half the people attending will be stopping by the grocery store on their way in."

Hands damp with sweat, Abby almost dropped Cole's plate of lemon squares on the cement entrance of the brick building as she tried to juggle her purse, the plate and the large metal door handle. Inside she could see people through the windows and hear the steady buzz of conversation. Her stomach twisted into a bunch of knots and her need to take flight almost won out over her need to fit in and belong.

"Need a hand?" A man in his early fifties with salt-and-pepper-colored hair stepped past her, pushed open the door and ushered her inside.

"Thank you." Even though Abby was only a few minutes late, a large number of people stood around in groups and filled the elementary school cafeteria. Some of them turned to look at the newcomers, others engrossed in conversation ignored them completely.

It was the first day of a new school all over again. Abby bit her bottom lip and looked around for a corner to hide in once she dropped off her plate. A stage with a mural of the school mascot and kids painted on the wall behind it filled one side of the room and folded up tables and benches stacked against one another filled another side. Colorful posters and phrases of encouragement lined three walls and windows made up the forth. No place to disappear. If only Cole had joined her today, but she understood his reluctance. Her wild gaze searched for Christine and came up empty. Now what?

"I don't recognize you." The man spoke again, his voice reassuring as he touched her arm and led her farther into the cafeteria. "I'm Jim Webb. I own The Thirsty Cactus restaurant and I'm the treasurer for the Chamber."

Abby breathed in a tentative sigh of relief. "Pleased to meet you. I'm Abby Bancroft."

"Charles and Sally's granddaughter. I'm pleased to meet you, too. Your B and B is my cousin's favorite place to stay when they come to town. I know they'll be glad to hear you're reopening it. How's the restoration going?"

"Just great. I'll be back in business by the Founder's Day Festival." Her steps faltered as they walked toward the row of cafeteria tables filled with food by the kitchen. No hint of judgment about her illegitimacy, just open friendliness. Maybe it didn't really matter after all.

Abby still felt that way an hour later when she'd passed out the last of the business cards she'd brought with her and had collected a number of ones for future reference. A smile lit her lips. She'd been accepted as part of the community. She finally fit in somewhere. Belonged. And it felt good.

Walking back to the food table, Abby made plans with the tall, thin woman who owned a knitting shop on the square to use some of her afghans in the living room. They filled their plates with more mini quiches, courtesy of Karin's Catering. Karin and Abby had hit it off instantly and had set up a meeting to talk about bartering for services. If things went well, Abby's guests wouldn't starve in the morning or be subjected to more burnt scones.

Abby left the woman by the vegetable tray and strolled over to the dessert section. Cole's contribution was a hit and the plate had only crumbs clinging to the floral surface.

"Abby, you have to give me this recipe." Mrs. Boyce, the owner of The Cowboy Exchange, another store lining Main Street, plopped the last piece of her lemon square into her mouth. "These are absolutely delicious."

"My contractor Cole Preston made them. I'm not very adept in the kitchen yet, but I'll get it from him."

"Is *he* still working for you?" Kitty Carlton, her grandmother's old housekeeper, announced loudly from the next group over. "Why Sally and Charles must be turning over in their graves."

Abby's fingers tightened around the foam cup of lemonade, threatening to punch a hole in the side. She blinked several times as she stared at the woman wearing a red suit that reminded Abby of a ripe, plump tomato.

The noise in the interior died down as if everyone waited expectantly for her reply. Abby's mouth flapped open, but the words in defense of her contractor stuck in her throat. She wasn't sure what she could say. He'd been right. Despite the work Cole had completed on her house, animosity remained when she mentioned his name.

"What makes you say that, Kitty?" Mrs. Boyce wore an expression of curiosity that brought a gleam to Kitty's eyes.

Her lips still frozen open, Abby sought for something to say that wouldn't jeopardize her acceptance in town. Apparently, bullying wasn't just a problem with the younger generation, but until now, she'd never been on the receiving end of it. Sure, kids had been mean and made fun of her while growing up, but they'd never downright attacked her for a decision she'd made. It usually hadn't mattered though, because in a month or two, she and her mom would have moved on to another place. Coward.

How many others in town felt the same way as Mrs. Carlton? Who else had the same thoughts hidden behind their welcoming smiles?

"Pay no attention to her, Abby." Christine moved in beside her and tucked her arm through Abby's. Cole's sister pulled her away from the table. "That spiteful woman has nothing better to do with her time than spread evil lies. My brother isn't the only one on her hit list."

Suddenly uncomfortable with the crowd and with her lack of defending the man she loved, Abby wondered how long she needed to stay. Despite the fact that most of them seemed to accept her and place no judgments, others like Kitty Carlton did. She'd hoped Dynamite Creek would be different. Uncertainty dogged Abby, making her long for the ocean and nothing between her and the water as she torpedoed over the waves.

Abby left Christine deep in conversation with Jim Webb and escaped into the cool breeze. Too bad she couldn't flee her thoughts as easily. Cole's kiss tormented her along with the faces of Kitty Carlton and the others who shunned her contractor.

Did Abby really belong here? Had her mother known something Abby hadn't figured out yet?

Two Fridays later, Cole sat down on the steps in the reception hall and sipped his coffee, waiting for Abby to return from her morning jog. Now that Cole, Robert and Abby had finished stripping the wood, tearing down the paneling and old wallpaper and fixing all the necessary repairs, they were ready to pull it all back together after they yanked up the rest of the carpeting.

The thick brew shocked his taste buds and jolted him to his feet when he heard footsteps on the front porch. He'd barely seen her since the kiss in the kitchen the day of the Chamber potluck, and he mentally kicked himself because he knew he was the cause of the shadows under her eyes and the disappearing act when he entered the room she was working in. Communication had been minimal, and Robert was usually there when they did talk.

Cole knew it was better this way, that his departure would end the tension between them because even though she hid her hurt, their connection made him experience the same emotions she did. Or suspected he did. He didn't want to, but he loved Abby. A future together was out of the question though. Despite his ex-partner's remarks, Cole wasn't the stick-around kind of guy Abby needed.

He opened the front door before Abby could figure out another way to avoid him and ushered her into the bare hallway. A healthy red glow graced her cheeks and he saw the look of unrestrained joy before her gaze clouded over and she tucked her emotions back into whatever box she kept them in. "Morning, Abby. We should be done restoring the place to its original glory and ready to bring back the furniture and stuff in about two weeks. You should have a few days to rest before you welcome your first guests."

"That's great. I never thought I'd see this day." She floated past him and twirled around on the tiled floor. Happiness radiated from her that Cole wished he could bottle up and take with him. "Thanks, Cole. For all your hard work. I would have never gotten this far without you."

"You're welcome." His fingers stretched out to push back the tendril that escaped her ponytail only to stop inches from her face when she finally stood still. He had no right to touch her again. Curling his short nails into his palms, he shifted to the side and hovered, unsure of what to do for the first time in his life.

Even God didn't seem to have an answer for him these days, yet He had to have some plan because He had led him here. Cole suspected it had nothing and everything to do with the woman who skittered away from him.

Abby popped her head inside the parlor and stared at the numerous cans of paint and stain waiting to be applied along with several rolls of silk wallpaper and changed the subject back to more neutral ground. "Too bad I couldn't find any pictures of what this place looked like right after it was built, but the archives in the museum only turned up the original plans and a picture of the exterior. I suppose I should've gone and tackled the storage room upstairs, but I had more fun poring over websites of Victorian interiors. I'm glad I decided to start from scratch. It'll make it seem more like mine."

"That it will. I also contacted the painting crew from Flagstaff we'd talked about earlier. They've got us slated for next week.

I need to finalize the colors with them. You want the house blue and the trim white?"

Abby nodded.

"Good. Robert and I will replace the sagging railing and the loose porch floorboards before they get here then. When do you plan on taking a look in the storage room for usable stuff? Christine said she could help tomorrow if you want her to. She has a good eye for decor."

"I dread going back up there. Tomorrow would work just fine. I'll give her a call later. Maybe I'll ask Helen and Betty, too. I know they've wanted to do something to help."

Relief and regret warred inside him. Without any further problems, Dynamite Creek would be a distant memory in less than three weeks.

Flipping on the light switch after lunch Saturday afternoon, Abby stared in dismay at the piles of boxes and old furniture in the large storage room on the third floor. Dread chased the moisture from her mouth. She'd peered in the room once when she'd looked over her inheritance with Delia and then again with Cole when they toured the house together that first day. "Now I know why I haven't come back up here."

"Wow." Next to her, Christine whistled

quietly under her breath. "It could take a week to sort through all this."

"Nonsense. We'll get this place sorted in no time." Helen dusted her hands together and moved out of the doorway to let Betty in.

Nicole bounded around them and jumped inside the room. "This is awesome, Miss Abby. It's going to be like a treasure hunt. I wonder if there are any old clothes and toys up here."

"I wouldn't be surprised, Nicole. If you find any, you're welcome to keep them if I can't use them downstairs. Apparently, my ancestors never threw anything away. I'm sure glad you guys could help today. Otherwise Cole would probably have to do a search and rescue later on."

"Not that he wouldn't mind, I'm sure." Betty leveled her know-it-all gaze on Abby.

Abby didn't have the heart to tell her neighbor that her thoughts were way off base. He'd kissed her, but Cole had no interest in Abby. At least not enough to stick around when the job was complete. "Where should we start?"

"How about over here and then we'll work our way back toward the window. If we can decide what furniture and other things could go downstairs, we can make more room to delve into the boxes. Since that's probably more personal stuff, you'll want to go through that by yourself."

"Sounds like a plan."

Twenty minutes later, the women had uncovered and pulled out two full-length mirrors, a footstool, a wingback chair and two stained-glass lamps. A pair of ornately carved end tables joined the growing stack of pieces in the smaller room to their right that would be taken downstairs once they were finished sorting. Another stack of broken odds and ends filled the small corner in the hallway to be disposed of in the construction Dumpster on the side of the house.

Christine leaned back on her heels and dusted her hands after retrieving a small cream and burgundy-colored vase with flowers painted on the side from a fairly good-sized box. "How beautiful this is. And your list of things to buy is dwindling quickly."

Abby breathed a sigh of relief. "That's a good thing. Even with Cole's discount at Lenny's, I went through far more money than I'd anticipated."

"That's not hard to do, especially since you encountered so many problems." Shaking her head, Christine pulled out two matching crystal candlesticks. "I have no idea why Charles and Sally would just dump this stuff upstairs and redecorate in the seventies."

"I have no idea either, but I'm glad they didn't get rid of anything. Some of it's beautiful."

"And some of it not so." Helen held up a porcelain pink shoe with a grotesque flower adorning the top.

"That might go in a bedroom, but definitely not on the main floor. Maybe the answers to that mystery are in one of these boxes, or in that secretary desk behind the two curio cabinets." Christine pointed to the piece of furniture they'd almost uncovered in the corner by the window.

"Mommy, look." Nicole pulled out a pair of white lace-up granny boots from an old steamer trunk. A hat with moth-eaten lace followed, and then a white dress that had faded to yellow.

"It's a little big, but I bet you could wear that as a costume," Abby said, glancing up from the porcelain mantel clock she'd just pulled from another box. One of the back legs was chipped but she'd find a place for it in what she'd called the burgundy bedroom directly below them.

"It looks like an old wedding dress. From

257

the style and size I'm guessing it's from the mid to late 1800s." Christine ticked off her fingers as she mentally counted. "It probably belonged to your great-great-great-grandmother or something like that. I wouldn't be surprised if we find pictures."

"Can I really keep it, Miss Abby?"

"Of course. I don't have any use for it." Abby knew she should feel something for the old dress, yet she couldn't connect with it. Not even when Nicole pulled out an oval gilded frame with a black and white picture of a serious-looking couple and handed it to her.

Christine took the photo and studied it before turning it over and pulling off the back. "I was right. This is Edith and Lewis Bancroft on their wedding day, June 23, 1877." She replaced the back and turned to stare at the front again, a frown pursing her lips, before she handed it to Betty.

"How dapper he looks and Edith was beautiful. Funny, I don't see any resemblance to you," Betty murmured and handed off the photo to Helen.

"I know." No tug of recognition grabbed at Abby but the picture would reside on the refinished mantel in the living room. Her future guests would love the family atmosphere within the home when she was finally done accessorizing the place. There had to be other photos around in some of these boxes. She'd have to make the time to look later, but she was still glad she'd decided to do her own thing in regard to the colors and wallpaper instead of redoing her ancestors' vision. Now that the hard part of the demolition was done, she couldn't wait to get started on the cosmetic work. After Helen gave her the photo, Abby moved it to the pile of stuff to be taken downstairs when they were ready.

"Looks like this is the last section over here," Betty announced. "I'm thirsty. I think I'll go downstairs and get us something to drink."

"Sounds good," Abby replied as she and Christine pulled an old dresser away from the wall that could be used in one of the bedrooms downstairs. A dust bunny kicked up and tickled the inside of Abby's nose, setting off a series of sneezes.

"Bless you."

"Thanks, Helen." Abby rubbed her nose and blinked away the moisture in her eyes. Now that they'd created a path of sorts, she gingerly stepped around more boxes, furniture and odds and ends and made her way to the east-facing window. Pulling off the dark sheet, sunlight streamed through the dirty glass. She turned around and saw the cavernous room in a different mind-set. "You know, this would make an awesome living space once I'm finally done downstairs. There's already a bedroom and a bathroom and I'm sure it wouldn't take much to convert the other space into a small kitchenette and dining area and a living room right there. That would free up another bedroom downstairs and give me a little more privacy."

"What about when you get married and start a family? I'm not sure this space will be big enough," Helen questioned.

Abby didn't miss the gleam in her neighbor's eyes. Disappointment pooled around her even though she knew it was for the best that Cole would be leaving in a few weeks. "That won't be happening any time soon."

"What won't be happening any time soon? How are you ladies doing?" Cole shouldered his way past an old floor lamp and another series of unlabeled boxes. He carried a tray with six glasses and a pitcher of lemonade.

Betty trailed behind him, her own eyes gleaming, as well. Abby suspected Cole's appearance was no accident.

Abby blushed, wondering how much Cole had heard. She wiped the bead of sweat from her forehead, picked up one of the cups and poured herself a drink. Unable to escape the confines of the space like she had for the past few weeks, Abby avoided his gaze, feigning interest in one of the rafters. "Oh, nothing. We're doing great."

"Good. Now that you're here, you can help move that big piece over there." Helen pointed to the large mahogany armoire against the wall before she forced her way into the conversation. "And we were talking about where Abby plans to live once she gets married and starts a family. I don't think this space is big enough."

"You're getting married?" Confusion and dismay distorted Cole's smile.

Abby's blush deepened and she wished the floorboards would break underneath her and drop her into the room below. "Eventually. Nothing immediate. Helen's got it all wrong."

From the corner of her eye, Abby saw Betty fold her arms under her ample chest. "No, she doesn't. We see the way you guys look at each other. If Cole would only pop the obvious question, everything would be okay."

"Can I be a flower girl?" Nicole piped in.

"No." Cole and Abby both spoke at the same time.

"I mean we're not getting married." Abby

rushed to the little girl with the crestfallen expression and gave her a hug. "I'm sure when your uncle does decide to in the future, he'd be honored to have you as a flower girl. It's just not going to happen quite yet."

Cole moved in next to Abby and ruffled his niece's hair. Even though he spoke to Nicole, his gaze never left Abby's face. Pain hovered beneath the wariness in his expression and Abby sensed it had more to do with his father this time instead of the working arrangement. "That's right, Nicole. You'd make a beautiful flower girl. There's just not going to be any weddings any time soon. At least not on this end."

Regret pounded Abby's heart even though Cole told the truth. She rose to her feet and moved toward the armoire. Her fingers touched the ornate carving of leaves on one of the front panels, the texture rough beneath her skin. Once dusted and polished, the piece would be absolutely stunning. She toyed with the idea of keeping it up here until she opened the door and immersed herself in the overwhelming scent of mothballs. Her eyes stung. Stifling another sneeze, she shut the door and leaned against the carved surface. "Anyone know how to get rid of that smell?"

"I'd try warm water and vinegar mixed with some baking soda. That combination works for a lot of stuff and it's not toxic," Betty piped in, her arms still folded under her chest. "Now, since I can't convince you two to tie the knot, let's keep moving on this place. We don't have much more time left before we have to leave, right, Helen?"

"Right. Let's get this thing moved so we can see what's behind it." Yet underneath her frown, Abby still heard her neighbor hum the wedding march.

Between all of them, they managed to scoot the armoire off to the side without scratching the floor or breaking anything from the antique. "Wow, that was heavy." Christine wiped her hands on her jeans. "I wonder how your relatives got it up here in the first place."

"A few strong men. Probably the same way we're going to have to get it down. Hey, what's that?" Abby spied some writing on one of the newly exposed wood beams.

Cole moved in closer, knelt down and rested his elbows on his knees. "Looks like one of your ancestors was into graffiti."

Abby joined him and traced her fingers along the scrawled initials. "I wonder who JLB was? And why would he be up on the third floor during the construction in 1885?"

He dusted a cobweb from her hair. "Some husbands built these homes for their wives as a wedding present. JLB is probably Jonathon Lewis Bancroft, the son of Lewis Eugene Bancroft, one of the founding fathers of Dynamite Creek. He made his money off the mines near Jerome."

For a fleeting second, the expression on his face conjured up an image that Cole was doing this for her as a gift, even though Abby was realistic enough to understand that this was not a wedding gift but an obligation he had to fulfill for his own sense of pride. Especially since they'd just agreed that they were not getting married.

"How do you know all this stuff?"

"We had to study it in history class in high school. Ms. Flynn was a stickler for detail. She's in her eighties now, but I bet if you went to see her, she could tell you everything you wanted to know about your ancestors," Christine piped in.

Filtered sunlight shifted inside the room casting it in a grayer shadow. Betty glanced at her watch and nudged Helen in the arm. She tilted her head toward the doorway. "Well, look at the time. We'd best get going. Dinner doesn't make itself, you know."

"I know," Helen responded, shuffling toward the exit. "Enjoy yourselves at the Crawfords' tonight, you two. They are such a sweet couple, newlyweds expecting their first child soon."

Abby wasn't looking forward to another dinner out, but she didn't want to hurt her hosts' feelings by canceling. She also didn't miss Christine's slight nod at the two elderly women before they disappeared. "Oh dear, Nicole, we've got to go, too. If you don't get through all this today, Abby, we'd be happy to come back and help after church. Will you be joining us tomorrow?"

Uncertainty formed in her stomach and hesitation had a lock hold on her vocal cords. Every Sunday she'd waited for that invite. And each week she'd breathed a sigh of relief, and she experienced that same feeling today, too. But this time she also felt a tug to learn more. "I . . . might. Thanks for the invitation. As for the rest of this stuff, I may lug some of these boxes downstairs and go through them after dinner. Thanks for coming over. Enjoy your new dress, Nicole."

"I will. Thanks, Miss Abby." Nicole bounded down the stairs after Helen and Betty. "C'mon, mom."

As if sensing the women's intentions, Cole retreated after his niece. "I'll go finish sweeping up in the bedroom before we need to leave. Call me if you need anything. Christine?"

"I'll be right down. Nicole forgot her shoes."

After Cole's tread on the wood stairs faded, Christine turned to Abby. "Don't give up on Cole, Abby. He's spent almost his entire life being rejected. Please don't do the same. You're the best thing that's happened to him in a long time."

CHAPTER ELEVEN

Abby had no intention of rejecting Cole. He'd already done a pretty good job of that himself by making sure she was aware of his plans to leave. Her shoulders slumped. He'd given her no choice and yet because she loved him, she'd let him go, this time making the choice herself instead of it being made for her.

Shoving all thoughts of Cole aside, Abby went straight for the secretary desk and opened the top glass doors. If she were to discover anything interesting, Christine was right, it would probably be in here. Nothing but two wood shelves, a few dust bunnies and the scent of old pine. Next she pulled down the center piece, and piles of old newspaper clippings and other papers spilled out of the various cubbyholes and scattered across the desk's surface. Nothing of interest unless she wanted to know what some of the household bills were from the 1940s.

The middle drawers revealed pens, pencils, a few scattered coins and paper clips. The two bottom doors only exposed old household ledgers and confirmed the fact that her ancestors never threw anything away, at least her more distant ones. Judging by the sterility of the rooms downstairs, her grandparents hadn't kept much from their time living here.

Abby tugged at a curl. Surely there had to be something. Her mother had grown up here, and yet it was almost as if she hadn't existed.

Sadness tugged her lips down. For years she had wanted a home, a place to settle down, and now that she had one, she couldn't reconcile her surroundings with a sense of truly belonging.

After lugging a few more boxes over to the door to take downstairs to sort through, Abby spied a white toy chest wedged against the wall. More boxes found themselves piled next to the others before Abby completely uncovered the chest. Her fingers trembled and her attempts to collect air in her lungs stalled when she read the name Sharon Bancroft scrawled in pink and red crayon across the top.

Her mother's things had to be inside.

Blowing away years of accumulated grime, Abby cautiously opened the lid and leaned back on her heels. The odor of mothballs assaulted her nostrils even more than the dust particles swirling around her head. A red rose corsage crumbled when she touched it, spreading its fragments across what looked like a prom program, the cream paper faded to yellow, the typewritten ink looked foreign compared to today's laser printing. Beneath that, a stack of yearbooks kept a few school newspapers from curling. Picking a paper up, she sat down on the floor and perused the articles, her mother's name on several of the bylines. Her mother had been a budding journalist?

Out of curiosity, Abby chose the top yearbook and leafed through the pages until she found her mother's senior year photo. Her hair feathered back away from her face in the Farrah Fawcett style and she wore a polyester blue shirt with a wide collar. A smile Abby hardly recognized grinned back at her as she traced the outline. She had her mother's eyes and nose, and similar hair color and saw a different version of herself.

She'd never seen a picture of her mother from her early days. Mom had nothing from her youth, almost as if she'd wanted to keep that part of herself hidden from Abby. Why?

Abby dove back into the contents almost hidden in the bottom, a large shoe box tied with a cream-colored ribbon caught Abby's attention. Pushing aside a tiny white lacy dress, a pair of baby booties, a ragtag blanket, Abby pulled it out.

Scooting back so she rested against the wall, Abby opened the box. Inside, a stack of unopened letters had been rubber-banded together and beneath them lay a faded baby book with silver lettering held together by a clasp. She tossed the letters to the side and forced open the clasp. A folded piece of paper slipped out, uncovering the photo of a tiny infant. Two footprints took up the bottom part of the page and the handwriting Abby recognized as her grand-mother's announced the weight and length of their new baby and a birth date that was five days later than the day her mother had always celebrated.

After unfolding the errant paper, Abby's eyes widened as she processed the informa-tion. The birth certificate in her hands shook enough to make a sound in the silent room. The sun had slanted over to the other side of the house, casting the room farther into the shadows. Abby thought she saw movement out of the corner of her eye, but when she glanced up, only darkness had crept in. She scrambled to pick up the stack of letters, her stomach unable to make up its mind if it would process or reject the lemonade Cole had brought up earlier.

Thumbing through them, Abby recognized her mother's writing on each envelope. "Return to sender." Pain clawed through her and ripped apart everything she'd known about her mother.

"Abby? Are you almost done? It's time to go." Cole's voice drifted up to her.

"Can you tell them I can't make it? I don't feel well." Somehow through her tears, she'd managed to sound normal. Or as normal as could be, considering that even though she carried the last name of Bancroft, their blood didn't run in her veins.

Seconds later she heard him ascend the stairs, concern weighing down his words. "What's wrong?"

Unable to talk now, yet grasping to contain her emotions, Abby thrust the birth certificate and stack of letters at him. She wrapped her arms around her legs, rested her forehead against her knees and rocked gently while biting her lip. She would not break down. She couldn't. Not in front of Cole. Feelings were a sign of weakness and got you teased and bullied in life. She wasn't eight anymore. She wasn't in California and Cole wasn't one of her classmates. She wasn't going to lose it but her tears threatened to spill over her eyelashes.

"What did you find?" Cole wedged himself closely beside her, his long legs eating up what little available space existed. He wrapped his arm around her shoulders and squeezed gently before he kissed the top of her head.

"The reason why I don't look like my ancestors." His warmth permeated the sudden chill inside the storage room and Abby lost the battle and found herself crying for the child she was and the woman she'd become. The release felt good but left her vulnerable and she wanted to cram everything inside and go back to the way things were before she met Cole, before she fell in love, before she unleashed these feelings that left her breathless and out of control.

Cole's breathing and the sound of rustling paper filled the area. "Your mother was adopted?"

"Apparently so. The last time I checked birth certificates don't lie."

"How did they manage to keep *that* a secret?" The rubber band broke when Cole scanned through the letters, his fingers finally resting on the first one. "This one was sent a few weeks after your mother left. Do you want me to open it?"

Abby nodded. She couldn't bring herself to do it, yet she needed to know what was inside. Cole rubbed her back and his voice broke as he read the words.

"My Dearest Sharon,

Please come home. We miss you. By now you've figured out your birth mother doesn't want any contact. We tried to keep in touch the first few years after we were blessed with you, but everything was returned so we quit trying. It doesn't matter anyway, because the moment I held you in my arms, you were mine. The answer to our prayers. The love of our lives. Our darling daughter that we love so much.

Your father has calmed down and wants you to come back. Right now we've told everyone you're visiting relatives in Los Angeles, but we won't be able to keep that up too much longer. Please come home.

Your loving mother, Sally."

Silence permeated the air around them, yet Abby didn't have the strength to lift her head. "Obviously my mom found out that her birth mother didn't want her but chose not to come back here. She had pride to a fault. Whenever she made a decision, she never looked back no matter who it hurt."

"I'm so sorry." Cole wrapped his arm around her waist again and gathered her close.

Abby relished the contact and buried herself deeper in his embrace. "My grandparents did try to find us. It wasn't them. It was my mom who cut all the ties." A hiccup interrupted her words and sadness streamed down her face as she clung to him. "She told me that she had no family. That it was just the two of us. That it would always be that way. And then she died. But she knew her adoptive parents were here and yet she never told me about them."

Her voice rose as her fingers bunched the front of his shirt. "She had to have received some of these letters. I recognize the addresses. Why? Why did she do that? Why did she send them back? Why?"

Abby fought to contain the blackness creeping along the edges of her consciousness. The dark tide crashed over her, carrying her helplessly along in its turbulent waters. What else had her mother lied about? Had Abby been adopted herself? Had Mom been wrong about God? Did He truly exist? Did she really want the answers to her questions when she was afraid of where the answers might take her?

Maybe it was better to go through life without knowing and living each day as it came, like now. Before Cole could answer, Abby changed her position and wrapped her arms around his neck. Her lips found his and with that joyous touch, forgot every reason why she shouldn't be comforted by the man she'd fallen for. Lacing her fingers through his hair, she pulled him closer, enjoying how he responded to her caress. Love splintered her every thought and action and she felt loved and cherished in return.

This was how it was supposed to be. Friendship, laughter, a dedication to a common goal and an undeniable attraction and love. This was the fairy tale she'd been searching for her whole life and until now had always been just beyond that next block or new neighborhood. Now that she held what she wanted in her arms, she didn't know what to do with it.

Abby broke free, her breathing coming in short gasps. Jumping to her feet, she paced between the window, the pile of boxes to be gone through and Cole. Tension ripped and shredded through the thick shroud she'd erected around her heart until nothing remained but the need to survive. Before Cole could destroy anything else inside her,

Abby balled her fists and kept her voice even despite the tightness. She'd broken down. No one had ever seen this emotional side that she'd always managed to keep hidden. She needed to retreat and take a moment to gather her composure. "I need you to leave now."

"What?" Cole's sudden pallor accented the dark circles under his eyes. He thrust his hand through his unkempt hair and stared at her, pain etched into every pore.

"You heard me. Please leave."

"You can't mean that."

Abby tried to put a cap over her emotions, but knew it would be impossible until Cole left the room. "I do. Please go."

"I guess it's goodbye then. Robert and the youth group can finish up the house now that the hard work is done. You'll still be ready in plenty of time. Good luck with your new venture." The harshness of his tone crashed over her as grief twisted his expression. He stood, reached out his hand, fisted it and then let it drop to his side. After one last look, Cole disappeared through the doorway, his tread soft and slow on the wooden steps that carried him away from her.

The finality of his words sunk in as the darkness scratching at the window matched the blackness inside her. Goodbye? What? He couldn't be leaving for good. He must have misunderstood her. Abby had only needed a bit of space. She hadn't meant forever. Running to the head of the stairs, Abby grasped the railing and leaned over as far as she dared. "Wait, Cole, come back. I love you. I didn't mean —"

A second later, she heard the front door open and shut. Gone out of her life like everyone else. It was too late. Abby had repeated the same process as her mother. Worse yet, she'd done exactly what she'd told Christine she wouldn't do. Abby had rejected Cole. She was no better than the townspeople or the other people before her.

Stepping back, she slumped against the unadorned wall and closed her eyes. She sank down into a sitting position and pounded her fists against her head as her tears flowed freely from her eyes. "Cole, wait. I didn't want you to leave forever."

What had she done? A few minutes later, she climbed to her feet and paced the area, her arms wrapped around her middle to protect herself. But how could she do that when she was the problem?

Abby stared at the letters littering the floor. She remembered her childhood and how her mom would waltz in and the next day they'd be moving somewhere else because she'd found a new man or a new job or whatever excuse she'd come up with. Moving on to something better instead of trying to make what she had work.

Now she understood. All the people in her mom's life hadn't left her by choice. Either her mom had left them or she'd pushed and pushed them away until they left. Abby didn't want to run anymore but she had no experience with permanence or how to achieve it. Was she kidding herself now? Did she have what it took for the long haul?

Pacing to the window, Abby plastered her face and hands against the cool glass and stared out past the barren branches just in time to see Cole exit his temporary apartment, march across the driveway and then jump into his truck. Despite the distance, the tension surrounding him cut through her and her heart ached at the anguish slashing his features as he twisted his neck around and stared up at the house before he slammed the truck door.

Slinking back into the shadows, Abby held her breath and wiped the moisture from her cheeks. He carried no suitcase or duffel bag, which sparked a flicker of hope, despite hearing him start his truck and pull out of the Wendts' driveway.

She didn't want Robert here. She wanted Cole. After running down the stairs, she hightailed it into her office and picked up the phone, but when dialing Cole's cell phone number, she heard his distinct ring coming from somewhere on the second floor. In his haste, he'd obviously forgotten to take it with him.

An idea blossomed inside her brain. Cole wouldn't even think of leaving town without his phone, would he? A smile hugged her lips as she tucked it inside her purse. Now she had to come up with a plan to keep him here permanently. For both their sakes.

Cole drove around awhile, his dim headlights barely cut through the shadows as he cruised up and down the main streets of Dynamite Creek. The action reminded him of his youth and all the mistakes he'd made and what he wouldn't give for a do-over. He'd make different choices, do other things and yet in the back of his mind, he knew this had been God's plan for him. Did His future plans mean for Cole to remain in town?

The thought didn't suffocate him like it once would have. Twelve years ago, he couldn't wait to put this all behind him. Tonight he couldn't begin to think about leaving it again. Funny how the years had added a quaint quality to the place he'd once called home.

Hunger forced him to search out food and he turned onto Elm Street and pulled into a diagonal parking spot to the left of the entrance of the Sunrise Diner. Gold lettering filled the wide windows and a flashing neon light announced they were still open just before eight o'clock at night. Jumping from his truck, Cole strode over to the glass door and pulled it wide. Jingling bells signaled his arrival as a gust of cool air followed him inside.

The sole occupant sat at the counter with his back to the door, but Cole would recognize Robert anywhere. Knowing it would be rude to sit anywhere else, he took a seat on the empty stool beside his ex-partner. "Hi."

Robert pulled the French fry away from his lips. "Cole? Not on a dinner date tonight?"

"No." Cole dumped out the packets in the sugar container, organized them and then put them back inside by color. "Abby wasn't up to it."

"So, why — ? Never mind. The cheeseburgers are good."

As Robert took a bite from his burger and chewed slowly, Cole's gaze skimmed the interior. The place hadn't change much except for a new coat of paint on the wall behind the counter. White Formica tables and red vinyl booths lined up two on each side of the door with six more hugging the wall behind him in the long, narrow space. Unlike some of the older buildings, the previous owners hadn't covered up the original brick, which added a certain charm and offset the faded black and white pictures of how the town used to look along with old mining tools and other ranch type items from days gone by.

"Sorry it took me so long, I was in the back doing prep work. I'm Katie, may I get you something to drink?" A blonde girl fresh out of high school stood behind the counter with a pad of paper in her hands. Her innocent eyes and light sprinkling of freckles across her nose reminded him of Abby.

Cole had it bad. It was going to take a long time to get over his former client.

"Iced tea would be great." He pulled out the laminated menu and stared blankly at the black letters before sliding it back in the metal stand behind the ketchup. Nothing would have any taste so it didn't matter what he ordered. Cole pointed to Robert's plate. "And I'll have what he had. Medium, no onions, please."

"Great. Mike will be glad to cook something simple. It is almost closing time, you know."

Closing time and no doubt the cute waitress had plans for the evening. Cole had no idea what fun was anymore since he'd been working on the Bancroft Mansion lately and before that cleaning up the mess left by the man sitting beside him.

Once Katie dropped off his drink, Cole picked it up and drank deeply. The silence between him and Robert deepened to suffocating and Cole pulled at the neck of his shirt. Without the work of the house dominating their stilted conversations, they had nothing left to say to each other. Cole should have found another place to eat.

"I'm sorry." Robert dropped the small piece of bun onto his plate and wiped his fingers with a napkin.

"For what?"

"For taking all the money and bailing on you. I wasn't in my right mind. Gambling made me crazy and I was so far in debt I couldn't figure a way out." He pushed the plate away, set his elbows on the counter and placed his chin over his clasped hands. "I doubt there's a way I can make it up to you, but I'd like to try."

Cole lowered his gaze from Robert's

stricken expression. A different type of emotion radiated from Cole's heart as the forgiveness he'd practiced washed over him, filling him with peace. Robert had come back and he'd brought money with him that had helped Abby with some of the expenses. He inhaled sharply as Katie placed his cheeseburger in front of him, his appetite resurrected.

"I'm willing to try again." Cole meant every word of it as he poured some ketchup onto his burger and then dumped some on his plate for his fries. Until the end, his partnership with Robert had been a good one. They'd complemented each other with their strengths and knowledge even though they'd kept their personal lives somewhat off-limits. That would have to change though. "When you're done here, we'll go back to the Valley and sort things out."

"When *I'm done?* What about you?"

"I'm leaving in the morning. With all the demolition accomplished, between you, Abby and the youth group, you should be able to get to the painting and wallpapering and anything else Abby needs to finish before opening day."

"You're leaving? Running like a coward? I'd expected better from you." Robert signaled for his check and pulled his wallet from his back pocket. "I'm out then. I plan on staying here. I thought you were, too, because the woman you love is here. Don't do something you'll regret later. I had a chance to take a hard look at myself while I was in jail and know what I want out of life. I just hope it's not too late to set things right."

Cole picked up his iced tea, but the cold liquid did nothing to alleviate the dryness and he set down the glass with a thud. His finger smeared the water condensation around the well-used Formica counter. His ex-partner didn't know all the circumstances. "I'm not running, Abby told me to go, so I'm only following her orders."

Robert set a few bills on the slip Katie dropped off, stood and strode for the door. Before he exited, he turned to face Cole. "I don't know what happened between you two but whatever it is, fix it. That's what you're good at. Don't waste ten years of your life trying to convince yourself it doesn't matter. Don't let her get away."

CHAPTER TWELVE

Abby woke up Sunday morning out of sorts from her fitful sleep. Darkness receded against the windows with the promise of a beautiful sunrise. Something was missing in her life and it wasn't just Cole. After she left a note on his truck, her strides ate up the sidewalk as she pounded out her much earlier-than-normal jog that should have made her feel better. Her brain still echoed with questions that repeated themselves, carrying the same beat as her shoes against the cement. Why had she ordered him to go? Why had he suddenly decided to listen to her? Nothing made sense anymore except the big hole in her heart. She was responsible for putting it there, no one else, so she had to be the one to fix it up.

Unlike her mother, Abby would swallow her pride and ask Cole to stay. Not just for her but for him. They'd accomplished so much, but still had a lot to do and she wanted him to see the finished product. If Cole left now, his actions would only feed into the negative rumor mill whirling around parts of town. If he finished the house, he could hold his head up high and put his past behind him.

All of his past.

"Morning, Mr. Barrymore." Abby waved at the white-haired man picking up the Sunday paper at the end of his driveway.

"Morning, Abby. How are things going?"

"Fine. Just fine, thanks. Have a great day."

"Thanks. You do the same." Mr. Barrymore grinned and nodded. "Oh, and can you ask Cole to stop by when he gets a chance? I have a small favor to ask him."

"I'll mention it when I see him." If it wasn't too late. If her contractor had decided not to leave without his cell phone that was wedged in her sweatshirt pocket.

The sun rose over the distant hill. Shafts of light streamed down, reminding her of a hazy picture from her youth of clouds and Jesus descending from Heaven, His arms open and welcoming to all. To her. She'd believed once and had opened her mind up during her time with Cole. Twice she'd even caught herself bowing her head and adding a silent amen to his mealtime prayer. Maybe it was time to rediscover her faith. It only seemed natural that Abby had to return to church and find God again. Another thing she had to be thankful to Cole for.

Sunday morning Cole shoved the last of his belongings into his duffel bag and did one last cursory glance around Mrs. Wendt's small apartment before he zipped it shut. It didn't feel right leaving the town he'd begun to think of as home again. It also didn't feel right leaving Abby. Letting her go was the hardest thing he'd ever had to do, yet he did it to protect her. No use giving her any hope there could be a future together, despite what Robert had said last night.

"You're a fool, big brother." Christine, who'd arrived moments earlier, moved from the doorway and jabbed him in the back before she tried to undo the zipper.

Cole loved his sister, but at times like this, she drove him nuts. Especially when he sensed a truth behind her words. He was a fool. Foolish for coming back in the first place. Foolish for thinking he would finally be accepted. Foolish for falling in love because in the end he'd wound up hurting Abby. And doubly foolish for thinking everything would be fine when he left.

"No. I'm being practical. Shouldn't you be getting ready for church?" Cole muttered, still trying to convince himself he was doing the right thing. Having his sister come here hadn't been part of his plan. He'd already visited his mother last night after he had left the diner, and then spent hours driving around to avoid seeing the lights on in Abby's house. He wanted to go to her then just as he wanted to go to her now. He loved her in spite of everything but he couldn't handle her rejection, so he had nothing else to do here but get in his truck out front and start the drive back down the hill. Duffel bag in hand, he spun on his heel to find Christine folding her arms across her chest and blocking his path.

"No. You're not. And I'm not going today. I think God will forgive me for not going while I'm trying to get you to change your mind. Abby loves you and you love her. What's really going on in that thick skull of yours?"

The silent treatment had never worked before so Cole had little faith that it would start working now. "Nothing but getting out and saving everybody a lot of pain."

He swept his free hand across his face and ordered the feeling in his stomach to subside. Had he been that transparent in his feelings? And what of Abby? Did she really love him like both Robert and Christine said? Sure she'd responded to his kisses and he'd noticed her gazing at him several times. She'd also allowed Robert into the house to help him because she'd been worried about his health, not just her timeline. Cole's shoulders slumped even farther. Love? He'd really made a mess of things.

"So you're running away, aren't you? Just like Dad. When things got rough, or not according to plan, he bailed. Like you're doing now."

"I'm not —" The truth hovered between them. Self-loathing weighed heavily on his mind when he realized both Robert and Christine were right. For years, he'd tried to avoid being his father only to realize that he'd followed in his footsteps. Okay, so he hadn't left a family behind, but back in Phoenix tucked in a box in a storage bin, Cole still kept all the postcards his father had sent over the years, each one from a different place, detailing his newest adventure. While Cole had chosen to stay in the same profession, he'd jumped from job site to job site without ever looking back.

Except this time. Instead of looking forward to the next project, he loathed leaving this one.

"You are. Don't you think Daddy's leaving affected his little girl, too? Do you think you're the only one who suffered?" She advanced on him again and wrapped her arms around his waist. "I need you to stay. Abby does, too. Get over it, Cole. I have. I would have thought by now you would have figured out that God wants you here. That's why He brought you back to us. Don't leave again. Don't make that same mistake twice. Please."

Tears spilled from Christine's eyes and Cole realized in his selfish preoccupation, that he hadn't thought about how any of this would hurt his sister or his mother. How his actions by lashing out at the injustice of his dad's defection had wounded the ones he loved, Abby included in that number and Cole, too, when he reflected on it. By running away, he'd only fueled his bitterness and anger. By leaving each time, he'd only denied himself happiness.

His dad had made his own choices. Cole could make his. He didn't have to make the same mistakes but did he have the courage to change?

The darkness receded a bit. Could he really stay in Dynamite Creek? Finally set down roots and have a permanent place to put his work boots at night? The thought didn't terrorize him like it had in the past and yet it couldn't be that easy. There was always a catch. Hushed whispers and stares haunted him. "But what about the animosity? What about the past and the people who don't want me here? I could jeopardize Abby's standing in the community if I stay."

"You're talking nonsense. Everyone was looking out for us, Cole, and they still are. That's what they do here in Dynamite Creek. Sure you're going to have the Kitty Carltons and other naysayers but you're also going to have the Dale Barrymores and the Lenny Keefers, too. They believe in you like I do. Like Mom and Manny do. Like Abby does. Please don't go."

"I have to. I'm sorry." Cole had made up his mind. He kissed his sister on the cheek and walked out the door.

As he headed to his truck, he noticed the white piece of paper tucked under his windshield wiper blade at the same time he realized his cell phone wasn't in his pocket. Dropping his bag onto the cement driveway, he pulled out the paper and unfolded it.

Cole, I have your cell phone and want to make sure to give it to you in person. Please stop by the house and pick it up. Abby.

Abby's floral scent tickled his nose and

his mind conjured up images of her from how she looked the first day they'd met, when they had gone sledding and then a kaleidoscope of various other pictures of her helping him around the house. Those things, her straightforward handwriting and to-the-point note made him almost forget his intention of leaving Dynamite Creek forever.

How could he walk away? How could he stay?

Forty minutes later, Abby sat in her car in the crowded church parking lot. She searched for Cole, disappointed that each white truck belonged to someone else. She had thought for sure he'd come to church this morning and had put his phone inside her purse. Maybe he'd ignored her note and left. Pain crushed her heart and made her dizzy. Her fingers bit into the fake leather around her steering wheel and her shoulders slumped, despite her survivor mentality. She'd get through this too, with the help of God. All she had to do was reach out and embrace Him and everything would be okay.

Inhaling sharply, she gathered her courage and stepped out onto the pavement. A feeling that she was coming home settled across her shoulders and stayed with her through the entire service despite the fact Cole never showed. Christine didn't appear either, but a lot of other familiar faces, including Robert's, greeted her and made her welcome.

No matter what happened when she saw Cole again, she'd truly found a home in Dynamite Creek. Abby bowed her head and said her own prayer after the pastor finished with the service. *Dear Lord, please watch over Cole and let him be happy. I hope he finds what he's looking for. Let him find the peace that I have. Amen.*

"Abby, we're so glad you joined us again today." Pastor Matt shook her hand in the hospitality room. His warm and inviting smile set her at ease and the butterflies in her stomach settled. Abby grinned back.

"It's good to be here." Daring to hope that Cole hadn't left yet, she wanted to put the other part of her plan in action because she wasn't going to fail. The only way to do that was to step out of her comfort zone and ask for help. "May I talk to you a second? It's about the house and Cole."

By 10:00 a.m. that morning, Cole paced the living room floor, glancing at his watch every thirty seconds. He'd driven around for thirty minutes after he'd left his sister at Mrs. Wendt's but couldn't force his hands to turn the truck toward Phoenix. He couldn't leave Abby. Not when they were so close to being finished. He'd never walked away from a project before it was finished and he wouldn't start now.

Where was Abby? Her note intrigued him, and he needed his phone. She should have been back from her run a long time ago. Frustration mingled with self-doubt and gnawed at his conscience.

He wiped the sweat from his brow, marched to the kitchen and emptied the contents of his coffee cup before rinsing it out in the sink and returning it to the dish rack on the counter. Any more caffeine would give him the jitters.

More than he already had at the thought of his upcoming conversation.

Nausea hit the back of his throat. What if she said no? Then he'd dragged his feet in leaving for nothing. Wrong. Abby was worth fighting for and he wouldn't take no for an answer. He paced into the parlor and started to re-sand a windowsill while he waited. The physical activity took the edge off the uncertainty of his future.

Thirty minutes later Abby waltzed into the room, her eyes bright and her cheeks rosy. She stared up at him with her exquisitely expressive eyes. How different she looked from the first time he'd met her and yet just as beautiful. They still had a few things to resolve, but he wouldn't let her get away from him. The hours they'd been apart had already been enough. "Where'd you go? I've been waiting for you."

"Hi, yourself. I went to church. I thought I'd see you there."

He turned to face her. His fingers itched to reach out and touch her warmth and press his lips against hers. The next few minutes would determine his future, their future — "What did you say? You went to church? By yourself?"

"I did. I tried calling both you and Christine, but since you left your phone here I had no way to get a hold of you. I'm glad you're still here to collect it." Abby inhaled sharply and stared at him through lowered lashes as she retrieved his phone from her purse. He sensed her sudden apprehension despite her generous smile as she handed it back to him. Her fingers lingered against his before she pulled away. "Too bad you missed the service today. It was an interesting sermon."

Hope blossomed inside Cole and the last barrier fell away from his heart. There was no way he could live without her smile, her generosity, or her belief in him. Daring to take the chance and believing she felt the same way, he gathered her in his arms, not surprised when she didn't resist and leaned into him. She felt right in his arms and in his life. "Really? What was it about?"

"Something about our paths in life and the number of people who pass through them. Some people stay, and others leave when we've learned the lesson they were meant to teach us. I understand that now. The only thing that is permanent is God and our love for Him. You know you don't have to leave. I didn't mean what I said last night. I mean I wanted you to leave, but not permanently."

Abby tilted her head back and looked at him, a hint of moisture touching her eyes. "I'm just not used to breaking down in front of people and showing emotion. I didn't know how to communicate that. I still don't but I'm trying." Inhaling sharply, she bit her bottom lip. "So here goes nothing. I want you to stay here with me. I don't think we're finished yet."

Cole grinned and nodded, his heart full of love and devotion. Robert was right. He wanted someone to love him and wasn't afraid anymore. "You don't need to be afraid anymore and neither do I. I know we aren't finished. And I'm not about to leave until the house is done, or ever. God isn't going to let us walk away from each other. Just because my father was a fool, doesn't mean I have to continue along that same path. You're worth fighting for. Every square inch of you on the inside and the outside."

Abby wrapped her arms around his neck and breathed in the hint of musk she associated with Cole. Her heart ached at the sight of the dark circles under his eyes and the pallor tinting his skin. He obviously hadn't gotten any more sleep than she had last night. His words finally sunk in. "You think so?"

"I know so." His fingers grazed her cheek before he claimed her mouth.

Abby gloried in his kiss, knowing for certain that she'd made the right choice in coming to Dynamite Creek and letting Cole and God into her life. A quick image of her mother danced in her consciousness but instead of pain, reconciliation took hold. Her mother had done the best she could, just as Abby was doing herself. Instead of pushing Cole away, Abby embraced him with all her heart as her lips responded to his caress.

Suddenly, a stream of water rained down on them, dousing them with cold and pieces of wet plaster. The sound of running water mingled with the tap, tap, tap of more water hitting the hardwood floor. The moisture permeated their hair and clothes and ran down Abby's cheek. The coldness shocked her compared to the warmth of Cole's skin.

"What's going on?" she murmured against his lips.

"Looks like a pipe burst." Cole tried to pull away, but Abby would have none of that. Not when she'd finally found what she'd been searching for.

"How apropos. What else can go wrong?" Abby laughed and pulled him closer and deepened the caress, paying no attention to the impromptu shower.

"A lot. I suspect God has made it certain I'll be sticking around for a while." Cole ignored the water and sprinkled Abby with more kisses.

"I wouldn't have it any other way."

"Oh dear. Excuse me." Helen's embarrassed voice infiltrated Abby's consciousness, as she tasted the promise of the future together with Cole.

"*Oh dear* is right. Er-hem, Cole, did you know there's a broken water pipe above your head?" Betty announced. Abby heard a slight scuffle and saw Betty try to pull Helen from the room. "See, Helen, I told you that we should have waited until later.

These kids obviously have other things on their mind."

"You don't say. I'm so glad our plan worked, with the help of the good Lord above, that is. The water is perfect. Couldn't have thought of a better way. We'd better get some towels though. Someone has to clean up the mess."

Cole reluctantly released Abby. He picked a piece of plaster from her hair before he leaned over and placed a kiss on her forehead. "Don't worry. I guess I'd better shut off the water before there's any more damage."

"A little water never hurt anyone, but I suppose you're right," she whispered.

Noise outside interrupted their lingering kiss. Abby turned toward the window and saw what looked like half the congregation, and then some, piled onto her kitchen porch and spilling out into the backyard. Pastor Matt caught her gaze and gave her a thumbs-up as the water quit raining down on them.

"Why are all these people here?" Wonderment filled his expression as red tipped the tops of his ears. "Do you suppose they saw us?"

Abby laughed again and wiped the dampness from his face. Her hands cradled his jaw, the day-old growth rough against her palms, which only made her more certain of her decision and her love. "My neighbors did. And I'm sure some of the rest of them did, too. Don't people who love each other usually kiss?"

"Are you saying what I think you're saying?" Cole rested his forehead against hers.

"I am. I love you, Cole."

Cole let out a cross between a laugh and a growl before he kissed her again. "I love you, too. Now can you please explain why all these people are crashing your house?"

"I brought in reinforcements to help us finish. I also wanted to show you that despite what you think, you are welcome here and that people don't hold against you what happened to my grandparents. Those that do we don't need in our lives anyway."

"You did this for me?"

Abby nodded. "I guess instead of a welcoming committee though, we'll need them for clean up now. Good thing we were here. No telling how much damage could have happened."

"True but I have no doubt no matter how bad it could have been, we'd get through it together. I wonder who shut off the main switch."

"The plumber did. Here are some towels."

Helen marched past them with an armload of towels, trailed closely behind by Betty. Their expectant gazes left no room for guessing their intentions. "We'll take it from here. You two get out of the house for a bit."

This time it was Abby who blushed. After another light kiss on the cheeks, Cole stepped away and ushered Abby through the kitchen and out onto the back porch. Sunlight surrounded them and Mittens wrapped his body around Abby's legs. Cole leaned over and scratched the tomcat under the chin, causing him to purr and cementing the tolerable relationship between them. Abby sighed, knowing neither one of them would wander around lost anymore because she'd opened her heart and her home to them.

Christine stepped away from the crowd and gave Cole a big hug. "I'm so glad you decided to stay. See, big brother. I was right. This is what people in Dynamite Creek do. They help each other. Care for each other. Love each other. Everyone is here to show their support. Why look at that, even Mrs. Carlton has come."

Abby's gaze froze on the older woman who wore an expression of moderate toleration as she gave them a tiny wave, a fraction of a smile creasing her red lips. Maybe there was hope for Kitty's housecleaning services after all once the B and B was open.

As the people gathered around them, Abby stared at Cole, her Prince Charming dressed in painters pants and a navy blue T-shirt. Fairy tales did exist. Happiness radiated from her as she wound her fingers through Cole's and inhaled his spicy fragrance. Her grandparents had given her so much more than a run-down Victorian. They'd given her hope for the future and a home to settle into and a place to fit in. All she had to do now was share it with the man she loved.

Epilogue

Four weeks later, Abby sat in the rocker on the front porch while Cole put the screens on the front windows. With the extra help from the congregation and the youth group, they'd managed to get everything done ahead of schedule, even the third floor living area she and Cole would share once they were married in June. All that remained was enlarging the kitchen, which would take place in the fall when business slowed down if Cole and Robert could squeeze in the time between all their other newly contracted projects. Until then, the Bancroft Bed-and-Breakfast had officially opened this past weekend and was sold out until after Labor Day.

The porch shielded her from the late morning sun, yet its rays still managed to glitter off her new engagement ring. No longer would fear shadow their hearts, only love remained. Mittens curled up at her feet and the only thing missing was a dog and a child or two, which would come in time.

"The place is just absolutely gorgeous, Abby. You and Cole did a great job." With a large present in her hands, Mrs. Gordon paused and let an overburdened Mr. Gordon descend the staircase with four matching suitcases.

"Thanks, Mr. and Mrs. Gordon. Shall I put you in for next year?"

"Absolutely." Mrs. Gordon stopped by her chair. "Your blueberry scones were exceptional this year. Even better than Sally's I must say. What's your secret?"

Abby stared at her fiancé's broad shoulders as he set in the last screen and smiled. "Cole kept me out of the kitchen."

"My, my. Did you hear that, Harry? A man who cooks." Mrs. Gordon winked at her. "He's certainly a keeper that one."

"Yes, he is."

"Here. This is for you. An early wedding present." Mrs. Gordon handed her the box with the silver wrapping paper.

"You didn't have to do that. Honestly." Yet Abby found the box on her lap. Gratitude for what she had and what lay ahead filled her, especially when Cole moved in behind her and placed his hands on her shoulders.

"Yes, we did. I saw it at the Dynamite Creek Arts & Craft show and knew it would be just perfect. This way I know we'll always have a standing reservation every year."

Abby protested enough to cause Mittens to jump up and scamper off the porch and into the bushes. "You would always have a standing reservation with us, but thank you."

After Abby ripped off the wrapping paper and opened the box, Cole reached in, unrolled the doormat and held it out. Underneath the painted picture of a cat that looked like Mittens, *Home Sweet Home* had been written in cursive.

Three little words that held so much meaning for both of them. Unafraid to show her emotions now, she felt tears form in her eyes. She stood and hugged Mrs. Gordon. "You're right. You have no idea how perfect it is."

QUESTIONS FOR DISCUSSION

1. In *Home Sweet Home,* Abby discovers that the house she has inherited isn't what she thought she was getting. Have you ever experienced a disappointment like that? How did you handle it?

2. Cole's faith helps him through his dark time when his partner took off with everything. Can you think of a time when you were down and God helped you through? How about how God works in the lives of your friends and family?

3. Abby is uncomfortable with Delia when she starts talking about God and faith. Is there another way Delia could have approached the subject? Have you ever been with someone who is uncomfortable with religion? How did you approach them and spread God's word and love?

4. Cole takes responsibility for his ex-partner's actions and completes all the jobs because he feels it will make things right with the Lord. Even though we are responsible only for our own actions, has there ever been a time when you have taken responsibility for someone else because you knew it was the right thing to do? How did it make you feel? Did it draw you closer to God?

5. Abby and Cole have differing views on how the house should be fixed up. What do they learn about each other while they work together? Do their different views help or hurt the project? Has this ever happened in your life? How did you settle your differences?

6. What is your favorite scene, and why? Your favorite character, and why?

7. When Abby attends a church service with Christine and Cole, she feels uncomfortable at first. Why? Have you ever felt afraid or scared of a new situation? How did you handle it?

8. Both Abby and Cole are scarred by their pasts. How did it affect their lives and

choices? Have you ever had something happen to you that affected the choices you've made? How did you handle them?

9. Abby has to learn to trust Cole with her house and her heart. Do you have trust issues? Has there ever been a time in your life where you had to put your trust in someone else? How did it make you feel? How did God help you with this?

10. Small towns like Dynamite Creek exist everywhere. What do you think the appeal is? What are the pros and cons of living in a small town? What about a big city or a rural community? Does where you live affect your outlook on life? How?

11. Acceptance is important to Abby because she's struggled to be accepted her entire life. Is there something you struggled with while growing up? With God's help, how did you overcome it?

12. Finding a permanent home is one of Abby's dreams. In the end, she realizes that it is allowing God into her life and the person she loves that make the home, not the physical location. Is there something you've always wanted to come into

your life? How has God worked in your life to achieve this dream?

13. When Cole and Abby suffer setbacks in restoring the house, she is ready to quit, but Cole won't let her. Has there ever been a time when you've had enough of a situation? What decision did you make? Did it make you happy? Would you make the same decision today?

14. After Cole leaves Abby, he realizes that by refusing to declare his love for her, he is denying himself happiness and rejecting what God has intended. Has there ever been a time when you rejected what God had intended for you? What happened? How did you make your peace with God?

15. In Luke 6:37, which this story is based on, it states, "Do not judge, and you will not be judged. Do not condemn, and you will not be condemned. Forgive, and you will be forgiven." This is true in our relationship not only with our family and friends, but with all of those around us. Can you think of the times in your life when you've had to apply this? How did it make you feel? How about the other person?

ABOUT THE AUTHOR

At twelve years old, **Kim Watters** fell in love with romance after she borrowed a Harlequin Romance book from her older sister's bookshelf. An avid reader, she was soon hooked on the happily-ever-after endings. For years she dreamed of writing her own romance novel, but never had the time until she moved from the hustle and bustle of Chicago to a small town north of Phoenix, Arizona.

Kim still lives in that same small town with her two wonderful children, one crazy dog and two high-strung hamsters.